'I know h
diggers.'

'It pays to be r...........................ptly.
The hard inflex...............made Roberta
shudder.

'I'll bear that in mind when I'm dealing with
your daughter,' she replied mildly.

Her eyes met his, and for the first time he
smiled. It lent his face such extraordinary
charm that she was almost knocked for six.

'I really would love to know what makes you
tick,' he commented lazily.

Dear Reader

Easter is upon us, and with it our thoughts turn to the meaning of Easter. For many, it's a time when Nature gives birth to all things, so what better way to begin a new season of love and romance than by reading some of the new authors whom we have recently introduced to our lists? Watch out for Helen Brooks, Jenny Cartwright, Liz Fielding, Sharon Kendrick and Catherine O'Connor—all of whom have books coming out this spring!

The Editor

Cathy Williams is Trinidadian and was brought up on the twin islands of Trinidad and Tobago. She was awarded a scholarship to study in Britain, and came to Exeter University in 1975 to continue her studies into the great loves of her life: languages and literature. It was there that Cathy met her husband, Richard. Since they married, Cathy has lived in England, originally in the Thames Valley but now in the Midlands. Cathy and Richard have one child, a daughter, Charlotte.

Recent titles by the same author:

CHARADE OF THE HEART
NAIVE AWAKENING

TOO SCARED
TO LOVE

BY

CATHY WILLIAMS

MILLS & BOON LIMITED
ETON HOUSE 18-24 PARADISE ROAD
RICHMOND SURREY TW9 1SR

*First published in Great Britain 1993
by Mills & Boon Limited*

© Cathy Williams 1993

*Australian copyright 1993
Philippine copyright 1993
This edition 1993*

ISBN 0 263 77974 2

*Set in Times Roman 10 on 12 pt.
01-9304-52206 C*

Made and printed in Great Britain

CHAPTER ONE

HERE at last. Dark, freezing cold, but for the first time in months Roberta felt some of that desperate unhappiness and awful, sickening sense of shame begin to lift from her shoulders.

She relaxed in the taxi, her eyes flickering interestedly over everything.

The taxi driver was chatting to her, capitalising on the fact that she was new to his city to boast about absolutely everything. And with good cause.

Toronto by night was marvellous. As the car weaved towards the heart of the city, there was something vital about the illuminated buildings that soared upwards, intent on reaching the stars.

In the distance, by the harbour front, he pointed out the magnificent CN Tower, the tallest free-standing structure in the world, and Roberta gasped in awe at the slender column, rising upwards to its distinctive bubble before narrowing to needle-like slimness as it stretched upwards. Look at me, it seemed to be saying; in this concrete jungle I am the undisputed king.

There was nothing like this in London. Roberta frowned. She didn't want to think about London. It made her depressed. She had come here in the hope of clearing her mind. The last thing she needed was to find herself pursued across the waters by her unhappiness.

'How long you over here for?' the taxi driver asked, and she dragged her attention away from the striking city skyline.

'A month,' she said. Would four weeks abroad really do anything?

'Funny time of the year to pick for a long vacation,' he responded, curiosity in his voice, and Roberta replied noncommittally, 'I don't mind the cold. It's refreshing.'

He smiled and fell silent, leaving her with her thoughts.

It still seemed an incredible piece of good fortune that she had managed to land this job, even though she was well qualified for it.

She had been doing au pair jobs for the past two years. It had started out as a way of earning money while she considered various other options, but she had enjoyed it so much that those various other options had gradually faded into the background.

She was, she supposed, suited to it. She was a calm, self-possessed person, and she had quickly found that her capacity for patience had a quelling effect on even the most brattish of her charges.

Her friends all thought that she was mad. Why, they had uniformly asked her when she had first started, do you want to waste your university education on looking after spoilt two-year-olds?

But now she was glad that she had done so. How else would she have ever got an overseas job?

Of course, this was a slightly different one from those she had previously had. Emily was no toddler. She was a fourteen-year-old girl and, from what Roberta had read between the lines at her interview at the agency, a rather lonely little girl.

No mother, father hardly ever at home. The sort of domestic background that bred problems. She was doubtless terribly shy and insecure.

She found herself drifting off into speculation, only realising that they had reached their destination when the taxi stopped outside the house.

Roberta absent-mindedly paid the driver and stepped outside, gaping at the massive edifice facing her as he carried her luggage to the front door.

'Well, have a good time,' he said cheerfully, and she nodded distractedly. She had known that her employer was wealthy, but she certainly had not been prepared for this degree of wealth. No wonder the child's father had no time for her, she thought wryly. He would have to work all the hours God made just to maintain a place of this size.

She tentatively rang the doorbell, hearing it reverberate distantly in the bowels of the house, and hoped that they wouldn't be too long because it was cold outside. A dry, biting cold which seemed to work its way through her layers of clothing until she could feel its fingers pressed against her flesh.

She shivered and was about to ring the doorbell once again when the door was opened by a middle-aged woman wearing an ill-humoured expression.

Roberta ignored it and smiled.

'Good evening,' she said as warmly as she could through chattering teeth, 'I'm——'

'Yes, yes,' the woman said, 'I know who you are. You're late. We expected you two hours ago.'

She ushered Roberta through, helping her with her cases, grumbling under her breath.

'I should have been home by now,' the woman muttered. 'I had to stay here with Emily.'

'I'm awfully sorry,' Roberta began. 'Surely Mr Adams——'

'Mr Adams works late most nights,' the woman cut in with disapproval in her voice.

'I see.' She didn't see at all. It was nearly ten o'clock, for heaven's sake! Apart from anything else, had he no interest in meeting the woman employed to look after his daughter? Rude, Roberta thought. A workaholic with no manners.

'I'm Glenda Thornson, by the way—the house-keeper,' the woman introduced herself, slightly less ill-tempered now that she could sense departure imminent on the horizon.

'Pleased to meet you.'

Mrs Thornson was already moving towards the staircase and Roberta followed her. 'It's a lovely house.'

'Not when you have to clean it.'

Roberta laughed and got a grudging smile in response.

She looked around her, appreciating the warm golds and yellows of the large hallway, and the tasteful inter-spersing of mahogany-framed paintings on the walls.

'Where is Emily?' She directed the question to the strait-laced back ahead of her and Mrs Thornson res-ponded without turning around.

'Asleep. Thank God. I'll show you to your bedroom and then, if you don't mind, I'll be on my way. Have you had anything to eat?'

'Yes,' Roberta said quickly, drily aware that any other answer would have met with a frosty reception. As a matter of fact, she wasn't terribly hungry anyway, even though she had eaten hardly anything on the flight over.

'Well, the kitchen is on the ground floor to the right of the house, and the fridge is well-stocked. There's some salad stuff, cold meats, and bread in the bread bin.'

They had arrived at the bedroom and Roberta stepped in, her face lighting up at the sheer luxury.

A huge bed, framed at the back by magnificent flowered drapes that fell to either side, dominated the room. On the floor, a massive rug picked up the colours of the curtains and the rosy tints of the antique furniture.

Mrs Thornson had retreated to the door and coughed pointedly.

'I'm just off, Miss Greene,' she announced. 'If you're sure that there's nothing that you want...'

Roberta smiled. 'A few hours' sleep might be a good idea,' she replied, just as eager to be on her own as Mrs Thornson was to leave the house.

'Fine. Well, I'll see you tomorrow, no doubt.'

With that she vanished, and Roberta carefully began unpacking, preferring to get it over with rather than be confronted with the task the following morning. Every so often she stopped to admire tiny details in the bedroom: the exquisite clock on the dressing-table, two small oval-shaped paintings on either side of the windows, the tapestry cushions on the bed.

Grant Adams clearly had taste, or more probably had paid someone who had to decorate the house.

The little touches, though, spoke of a female touch. Was this how Emily spent her time when she was not at school, perhaps? Trying to instil atmosphere in a place which, if left to her workaholic father, would have no doubt been an empty shell?

Roberta had seen enough of workaholics in her job to know that they rarely noticed their surroundings. They were invariably middle-aged men, their faces creased with lines of stress, who only seemed to come alive when discussing their work.

She was about to stick her suitcase into the wardrobe when a girl's voice said from behind her, 'So you're the au pair grandmother insisted on importing.'

Roberta spun around. This was certainly not the child she had imagined. Long, black hair fanned out around a face that was sullen and suspicious.

'Yes, I'm Roberta Greene and you must be Emily,' she said, rapidly realising that this girl definitely did not while away her spare time adding female touches to the house.

'Who else?' She strolled into the room and sat on the bed, idly fingering the remnants of clothes to be stored away and staring openly at Roberta.

'I'm sorry, I would have looked in on you but your housekeeper told me that you were asleep. It's a pleasure to meet you at last.' Roberta smiled.

'No, it's not.' Green eyes narrowed on her with biting dislike. 'Not for me, anyway.'

'Then why,' Roberta continued in the same polite voice, 'did you agree to having an au pair?'

'It was you,' Emily responded sourly, 'or my vile re-lations in New Hampshire. I wanted to go to Europe with Grandmother, but she refused. I suppose she thought that the next best thing was a European au pair.' She gave a short laugh. 'Or maybe she just thought that once you were over here it would be more difficult for you to leave.'

'More difficult for me to leave?' Roberta repeated warily.

'Sure. The last two au pairs I've had didn't last a week, never mind four.'

This, Roberta thought, removing her clothes from within Emily's reach, was not what I had expected.

'What did you do to them?' she asked mildly. 'Frogs under the pillows? Buckets of water in strategic positions?'

'Don't be ridiculous!' Emily's face flushed. 'I'm not a child!'

'Aren't you? Silly me, I thought you were fourteen. The interviewer at the agency must have got it wrong.'

'Very funny,' Emily snapped, but there was reluctant interest in her eyes now. 'Is that a British sense of humour? I suppose you think you're clever, do you?'

'Not at all!' She sighed and looked calmly at the girl. 'Look, we're going to be together for the next few weeks. Why don't we call a truce and try to be friends?'

'Friends?' Emily sniggered. 'I may be stuck with you, but that certainly doesn't mean that I intend to become friendly with you.' She stood up, and pulled her dressing-gown tightly around her angular frame.

Her little hands were clenched around her, and Roberta saw that the knuckles were white. Much as she wanted to pose a threat, Roberta could see that underneath she was little more than a defensive child. A product of her upbringing.

She felt a surprising twinge of anger directed against the child's father. Couldn't these sort of people see the effect that their obsession with work had on those closest to them?

Emily was still scowling at her, and she glanced at her watch. 'Perhaps you'd better be off to bed now. We can continue this discussion in the morning.'

'Don't worry. That's precisely where I intend going. I just thought that I'd come and check you out myself.'

'I'll see you tomorrow, Emily.'

The sentence was scarcely out of her mouth before the girl had flounced outside, slamming the door shut behind her.

Oh, lord, Roberta thought, sitting on the bed, this is definitely a far cry from a spoilt toddler who could be appeased with ice-cream in the park and trips to the zoo.

She tried to remember what the interviewer had said about Emily. Very little, from what she could recall, apart from the barest of facts. That she was fourteen, and lived with her father and her grandmother, and that she was between schools.

And Roberta had asked very few questions. She had been so keen to get the job that she had accepted what she had been told rather than miss the opportunity to leave England by appearing too inquisitive and choosy.

For instance, where was the mother? Were Emily's parents divorced, perhaps?

She was beginning to get a headache from thinking about it, and on the spur of the moment she hurried downstairs, tentatively making her way towards the kitchen.

Like the rest of the house, it was sumptuously fitted out. The counters were a mixture of frosted oak and multi-coloured granite, and overhead a hanging shelf supported a range of plants which trailed downwards.

She poured herself a glass of milk and settled at the round kitchen table to drink it, mulling over in her head what other surprises lay in store for her.

Perhaps a few vicious Dobermanns that the interviewer had also failed to mention? She grinned to herself, feeling decidedly better now that there was something in her stomach.

It suddenly struck her that she had not given any thought to her own problems ever since she had stepped foot into the house. Maybe a difficult teenager was just the tonic she needed, she thought. Not that Emily was difficult. Probably just unhappy. She glanced around her and thought how lonely it must be for a young girl to be surrounded by such vastness, a vacuum which surely an ageing grandmother and a father who was absent most of the time found impossible to fill.

She carefully washed her glass and was heading back to the bedroom when the front door opened. Or, rather, it was pushed open forcefully, and the sight of a man framed by the blackness outside, the biting wind blowing his black coat around him, made Roberta's blood freeze in her veins.

She had never been confronted by a more alarming sight. The sheer height and power of the man startled her, and it wasn't helped by the expression of aggression on his face as his eyes raked over her mercilessly.

He slammed the door behind him without taking his eyes off her and slipped off his coat to reveal a superbly tailored grey suit, which somehow did nothing to lessen the impression of savage power that had initially struck her.

Roberta remained standing where she was, glued to the spot, too terrified and fascinated by the vision in front of her to move a muscle.

Then he spoke, and it struck her that his voice somehow matched the rest of him. Deep but hard, with a hint of menace behind it.

'Is this some kind of joke?' he asked grimly, striding towards her.

Roberta cringed back, her eyes wide, her self-control for once deserting her. Alarm had replaced reason and her mouth was half parted in fear.

Her brain had somehow started functioning again, though, enough for her to recognise after the initial shock that this must be Emily's father. The same dark, almost black, hair, the same peculiar shade of green eyes, but his features were harsh and arrogant. It was a striking face, one that forced you to look at it, and which, once seen, was never forgotten.

'I asked you a question,' he bit out. He was close to her now, towering above her. With a swift movement, he reached out and grasped her by her arm, shaking her out of her immobility. 'Who the hell are you? Some friend of Emily's? Is this my daughter's idea of a sick joke?'

Anger suddenly replaced fear and Roberta's lips compressed tightly. 'You're hurting me,' she said icily, but, instead of that having the desired effect, he shook her again, sending her hair flying around her face.

He's mad, she thought with a jolt of panic. I've managed to land myself a job looking after a wayward teenager with an insane father. Why else would he be behaving in such a bizarre fashion?

'If you don't let me go at once, I'm going to scream,' she said unsteadily, staring up into his ferocious green eyes.

'Is that a threat? Because if it is, you seem to have forgotten whose house this is.'

His voice now was quite calm, but all the more disturbing for that.

'Now, are you going to tell me what's going on here, or do I have to shake it out of you?' His voice left her in no doubt that he was prepared to do precisely that and she shivered.

Common sense told her to hang on to her self-control, but something about this man, quite apart from his behaviour, unsettled her. Everything about him was overpowering.

'I'm Roberta Greene,' she replied as calmly as she could, feeling like someone who had suddenly found themselves in a lion's den and was trying to find the right placatory tone of voice to enable them to leave in one piece. 'I'm here to look after your daughter.'

There was a long silence while he surveyed her at leisure and with the same glint of ruthless hostility in his eyes.

'Well, Miss Roberta Greene, I don't know how you managed to land this job, but you can forget about unpacking, because you're going to be on the next flight out of here.'

'What?' Roberta looked at him, confused. 'Why? What are you talking about?'

He gave her a scathing look and then proceeded to half pull, half drag her towards the massive left-hand wing of the house, into which she had not ventured.

Roberta wriggled against him, desperately trying to free herself from his iron grip, but it was useless. She was no match for his strength, and in the end she abandoned the effort, her mind whirling in confusion.

What was going on here? I should never have accepted this job after all, she thought, I should have known that it was too good to be true. Doesn't fate make a habit of tripping you up?

Something was terribly wrong here. There was no way that this man's behaviour could be classified as normal.

She was suddenly aware of the silent spaciousness around her.

'Where are you taking me?' she asked, her voice uneven from the exertion of keeping pace with him.

'Don't you know? I'm sure you can suspect.'

He pushed open a door on the right and switched on the light, which threw the room into instant clarity. It was a large den. In one corner there was an old-fashioned desk with a computer terminal perched incongruously on top of it and the walls were lined with bookcases which groaned under the weight of books of every description.

'Well, Miss Roberta Greene,' he addressed her tightly, swinging her around, 'tell me that this is a shock to you.'

Roberta stared in front of her at a large portrait which had not been visible from the door. It was of a woman of a similar age to her, wearing a forced smile on her lips.

'Who is it?' she asked, curiosity overcoming her confusion.

'My wife, as you well know,' he said derisively.

'Why should I know?'

'Don't tell me that it was sheer coincidence that you applied for this job. Look at the portrait. Can't you see the resemblance?'

Roberta focused on it and she reluctantly saw what he meant. They both had red hair, pure natural red, unadulterated by any shade of brown or auburn and, from what she could see, the same grey, widely spaced eyes.

But there any resemblance stopped. Roberta's hair was cut in a neat bob that hung to her shoulders, and far from being neat and plain, which was how she considered herself, there was something untamed about this woman in the portrait. Her hair was a mass of curls, her eyes wild and knowing.

Was this what lay behind his accusations?

'What are you trying to imply?' she asked coldly, turning to face him. Her colour had returned to normal, and that alarming, addled feeling she had had a moment ago had subsided.

'Put it this way,' he said in an unyielding voice. 'It isn't the first time that someone has tried to wheedle her way into my affections, or should I say my money, by playing on a resemblance to my late wife.'

Roberta stared at him, taking in the hard contours of his face. Was there any woman brave enough to try and wheedle her way into this man's affections? she wondered. He didn't strike her as the sort who could be wheedled into anything. In fact, he looked the sort who played situations to suit himself, and to hell with the rest of the world.

'Late wife?'

'Yes, late,' he snapped impatiently. 'She died some years ago.'

'I'm sorry.'

'So am I. Sorry that you turned up here.'

'I'm afraid you're quite wrong about me,' Roberta informed him calmly.

'Oh, are you really? Afraid that I'm quite wrong about you?' He stared back at her until she flushed, and then the harshness in his face softened slightly into amusement.

Roberta felt a surge of anger which she quickly stifled. She could see what he was thinking clearly enough because he couldn't be bothered to hide it. He saw her as a prim little English woman, with nothing of that tigerish grace of his late wife, and he found it laughable.

She didn't care, but on the other hand she didn't see why she should have to put up with being the butt of his humour merely because he happened to be her employer.

'Quite frankly, and I'm sorry to dent your ego, I had never heard of you until I applied for this job.'

'I may be Canadian,' he drawled, 'but my face is well-known in the business circles in your country. As was my wife's.'

She detected a certain inflexion in his voice at the mention of his wife and she put it to the back of her mind.

'I don't know a great deal about business,' Roberta said, folding her arms across her chest and not caring for the way he raised one eyebrow at the movement. 'I'm an au pair, not a stockbroker. I really wouldn't know a prominent businessman from a bank clerk. I also,' she continued, irritated with herself for being addled by those brilliant-green eyes, 'consider it very rude that you haven't seen fit to introduce yourself.'

'Are you usually so uptight?' he asked, ignoring her question and moving to sit in the leather armchair, where he proceeded to scrutinise her with infuriating thoroughness.

'I've just been dragged through your house,' Roberta replied through gritted teeth, 'subjected to wild accusations—naturally I'm a bit tense at the moment.'

'Naturally.' He was laughing at her, even though his face was serious.

'And you still haven't introduced yourself,' she flared. 'I take it that you're Emily's father.' She knew who he was, of course, but that didn't mean that it excused his lack of manners.

'You're like a schoolteacher I once had,' he said, ignoring her yet again. 'Very prim and always bristling with righteous indignation.'

Roberta was positively fuming now. She hardly ever got angry, but right now she felt like exploding.

'I seem to remind you of a lot of people, don't I?' she intoned politely. 'I had no idea the world was so full of my look-alikes.'

He laughed at that, and her lips tightened a little bit more.

'Definitely like that schoolteacher I mentioned,' he said, 'and the name is Grant Adams.'

Without that hostility marring his features, she was disturbed to realise, there was something very attractive about this man. Maybe it was that combination of striking good looks and the sense of power that he radiated.

Either way, it alarmed her, because after everything that had happened she should be immune to men, most of all men with charm.

They were dangerous, and danger was one element in her life she could quite happily live without.

'I wish I could say that meeting you has been a pleasant experience, Mr Adams,' she heard herself saying, 'but I can't.'

'Let's hope that time remedies that,' he murmured, his eyes still glinting as though he found her a diverting novelty. 'Have you met my daughter?' He waved her to the other chair in the room and she hesitatingly sat down.

She had hoped that she might be able to leave the room, but he was clearly not in the slightest bit tired. In fact, he looked as though he could have kept going for another few hours at least. If this was his norm, then lord only knew how much sleep he needed. Maybe none. She glanced across at him and decided that he was the type who considered sleep an unnecessary waste of valuable time.

'Briefly,' Roberta replied. 'I'm afraid I was a little late getting here, and she was in bed when I arrived, although she did pop into see me.'

'I can imagine,' he said blandly, 'and what did you think of her?'

'She seems very outspoken,' Roberta said carefully.

'I would say that that's an example of very British understatement. She lacks discipline.'

'Lots of teenagers are a bit unruly, Mr Adams.'

'Grant. And Emily goes way beyond the boundaries of unruly. Have you been told that she's been expelled three times?'

'No,' Roberta admitted, not surprised at that.

'Have you been told that she should be at school now, but she was expelled from her last one a month ago?'

'No.'

'That hardly surprises me. My mother probably thought that such vital statistics would put off any prospective candidates for the job. Not many people are ready or willing to take on a fourteen-year-old with no sense of responsibility.'

Roberta was shocked by the inflexible hardness in his voice. No wonder your daughter's a bit off the rails, she wanted to say.

'A sense of responsibility is something that's gleaned from the example of those around,' she said bluntly.

'Meaning?'

There wasn't a great deal of amusement in his eyes now. She suspected that he was not accustomed to being criticised, however implicitly, and he didn't like it.

'How much time do you spend with her?' she asked, and his frown deepened.

'Excuse me,' he said coldly, 'but who's employing whom? I don't like your tone of voice, and I certainly don't like what I think you're saying.'

'I'm sorry,' Roberta murmured, not feeling sorry in the slightest. 'I don't mean to tread on your toes, but from what I gathered you don't spend a great deal of time with your daughter. If you did, perhaps she might be more inclined to live up to your expectations of her.'

'In case it hasn't occurred to you,' he said in a hard voice, 'I do have a living to make.'

'But at the expense of your daughter?'

'What?' he roared, running his fingers through his hair and glaring at her. 'Have you forgotten that you're paid to look after my daughter and not to analyse my behaviour?'

'I'm sorry,' Roberta said calmly.

'You don't sound it!' He stood up and paced the room to the window, staring outside, his back to her.

No, she thought, he really was not accustomed to being criticised. No doubt that was something he held the monopoly on. And got away with, judging from what she had seen.

But his air of restless aggression didn't intimidate her. When it came to her job she was coolly professional and daunted by very little. It was only in her personal life that she had bumped into things she couldn't handle.

'I was wrong about you,' he bit out, turning to face her. 'You may have a passing resemblance to Vivian, but that's about all.' He walked across the room and leant over her, his hands gripping either side of the chair. 'But something must ruffle that cool exterior of yours. What is it? What goes on behind that controlled face of yours? You've made your opinions of me loud and clear; now it's time for me to ask a few questions. After all, I'm entrusting my daughter to you.'

CHAPTER TWO

ROBERTA regarded him with a trace of alarm. As far as she was concerned, being au pair to Grant Adams's daughter in no way gave him an invisible right to quiz her on her personal life, but the look of intent on his face, inches away from hers, disturbed her.

She lowered her eyes and wished that he would remove himself to another part of the room. His daunting masculinity so close to her made her feel slightly giddy and out of control and she didn't like it.

'I don't think,' she said carefully, 'that what goes on under this cool exterior of mine, as you put it, has anything to do with my job here. I'm being paid to look after your daughter for four weeks, and that's precisely what I shall do. I happen to be very good at my job.'

'I never said you weren't.'

She could feel his breath warm on her face, and it seemed to go to her head like incense. That, coupled with the relentless, demanding glint in his eyes, made her hackles rise even further and she had to control herself against another unaccustomed surge of anger.

'Then I don't see that there's anything further to discuss,' she said evenly, raising her eyes to his.

'You really would have made a great schoolteacher.'

'And I resent your constant insults!' she snapped.

'Me? Insults? I thought that you were the one doing that.'

'What do you mean?' She eyed him levelly, inwardly cringing from that intangible sense of unquestioned power that radiated from him.

'What I mean, my dear Roberta Greene, is that you feel free to make sweeping generalisations on my relationship with my daughter, but the minute I suggest that I try and discover what makes you tick, you instantly clam up. Surely you can see it from my point of view. I know nothing about you.'

'I come with references,' Roberta interrupted him, realising that her choice of words made her sound like some kind of prize dog proclaiming its pedigree. 'Your mother will have copies of them all——'

'But what do they say about you?'

'That I'm experienced in this,' she said evenly. 'I've been an au pair now for two years. There's not much else I can tell you, except that you must trust me with Emily.'

He stood up and walked back to the armchair by the desk, and Roberta breathed a sigh of relief. She hadn't realised how much she had been affected by his proximity until she felt a swift release of tension that made her body sag.

Poor Emily, she thought sympathetically. She was probably scared stiff of her father. He certainly didn't seem the sort who had a great deal of patience, and that was the one virtue that most adolescents needed in abundant supply.

'I don't suppose I have much choice, do I?'

It was a rhetorical question, but Roberta answered it nevertheless.

'You could always ask me to return to England,' she pointed out. 'After all, you didn't hesitate to do that when you thought——'

'When I thought that you had conned your way over here on your physical similarity to my wife,' he finished for her, and she nodded. He shrugged. 'I know how to handle gold-diggers,' he said abruptly. 'It pays to be ruthless.' The hard inflexion in his voice made her shudder.

'I'll bear that in mind when I'm dealing with your daughter,' Roberta said mildly.

Her eyes met his, and for the first time he smiled, a genuine smile that lent his face such extraordinary charm that she was almost knocked for six.

'I really would love to know what makes you tick,' he commented lazily, and she stood up, in no way prepared to let his idle musings force her into a position of defensive anger again.

She didn't need anyone prying into her life. Right now, it was all too sensitive a subject for that. Not that she would have been inclined to have told him anything, anyway. She was not given to sharing confidences, least of all with a man who gave off warning signals that even a deaf person would have been able to hear.

'And I really would love to get some sleep,' she said politely, with a cool little smile on her lips.

'I take it that was a "hands off" remark?' he asked with amusement. Any minute now, Roberta thought with hostility, he'll start referring to me as quaint, or an oddity.

'If by that you mean that I don't intend to discuss my personal life with you, then yes, you're absolutely right.'

She began to move towards the door when his speculative drawl stopped her in her tracks.

'Same colour hair, same eyes, but you really are nothing like my late wife at all. Unless, of course, you're an extremely fine actress.'

Roberta didn't turn around. She found his words offensive, because when she thought of that woman in the portrait she thought of everything that was wild and exciting. To have the differences between them pointed out to her was tantamount to telling her that she was as dull as dishwater.

Nobody likes to think that they're dull, do they? she told herself.

'If I were an extremely fine actress,' she said, staring straight ahead of her, her back to him, 'I wouldn't be an au pair. I'd be in the acting profession.'

'I hope so,' he said, conversationally enough, 'because, as I said, I can be ruthless when it comes to gold-diggers.'

There was no answer to that one, and Roberta left the study, shutting the door quietly behind her, quickly running up the stairs until she got to her bedroom.

It was late, and she hadn't slept for hours, what with the long flight and the inevitable waiting around at airport terminals, but she didn't feel tired at all. Her mind felt as though it had been suddenly thrust into overdrive, and as she undressed and lay on the huge bed her thoughts flitted tantalisingly and aggravatingly back to Grant Adams. Odious man. Not only had he seen fit to insult her, but he had also seen fit to laugh at her.

She had only met a few North Americans in her life. They had been full of *joie de vivre* and terribly extrovert. She wasn't like that, but her natural reserve wasn't a matter for amusement, was it?

She had always been quite reticent. She wondered now whether that hadn't increased over the past eight months.

She cast her mind back over everything that had happened to her recently, for the first time not feeling her stomach contract at the thoughts racing through her mind.

Her mother's death she could face now with less of that desperate sense of loss. The pain was duller, more of a lingering sensation of sadness.

She had been very close to her mother. From as far back as she could remember they had been a twosome. Her father had died when she was only eighteen months old, and her mother had never remarried.

'It could never be the same,' she had once told her. 'I loved him too much to ever give my heart to someone else. It would have seemed like a betrayal.'

So they had tackled life together, hand in hand, and when she died quite suddenly nine months ago Roberta had been shattered.

Now, looking back, she could see that Brian's entrance into her life had come when she least needed it. She had been vulnerable, unprepared, emotionally in need of support, and he had swept through her like a whirlwind. Blond, handsome, charming, he had wooed her with flowers, surprised her when she least expected it.

Roberta stared upwards at the ceiling, allowing her mind to roam freely for the first time over her huge mistake, not trying to shut it away somewhere safe where it couldn't touch her.

We all make mistakes, don't we? she told herself.

How was she to know what he really was? She had had no experience of men, after all. Physically, her life had been a closed book as far as that was concerned. When he didn't pressure her into sleeping with him, she had been relieved and delighted. It had been one more point in his favour, so his requests to borrow some money, small amounts to start with, had hardly caused a ripple.

He had told her that he was an actor, struggling to get parts.

Now, as she lay in bed, she found that she could actually think of his lies with a certain degree of resigned cynicism, instead of with that choking bitterness.

Of course he hadn't been an actor, though he should have been one. His performance with her was deserving of an Oscar. He had softened his borrowing with little, thoughtful, romantic gestures, and like a fool she had swallowed it all hook, line and sinker.

She had let herself be lulled into a false sense of security, had even begun discussing marriage, and he had encouraged her in that. So, when he raised the subject of buying a house together, it had seemed reasonable enough to her. He had persuaded her that she could keep on her mother's place, renting it out, as an investment, and they could use the better part of the money left to her to buy into a new property.

They would be cash buyers; they would have no problem finding somewhere. The market was depressed; they could find a bargain.

His arguments rang in her ears as though they had been spoken just yesterday instead of three months ago.

And she had fallen for them.

'You make the cheque over to me,' he had told her. 'I have some money of my own in savings. I'll make one cheque out to the solicitors. No point in creating unnecessary paperwork.' He had worked out in detail how much money they jointly had, and his tone of authority, his tender, clucking dismissal of her shadowy doubts had persuaded her in a way that nothing else could have.

The memory of it made her flush with bitter shame. How could she have fallen for someone so obvious? But she had. Like a naïve fool, only realising that she had made a massive error of judgement when he abruptly vanished from her life. She had tried calling him, but the number had been disconnected. She had gone round to his bedsit, but he had flown the coop.

The new tenants had stared at her and shrugged their shoulders. This was London, they had said, of course we don't know where he's gone, we were only happy to have got the flat.

Disillusionment had given way to anger, and then to bitterness. Of course, she had eventually gone to the police, but by then she had resigned herself to the fact that she had kissed sweet goodbye to her money.

She could recall the interview with the chief inspector in minute detail, and it still had the power to make her cringe. She had known precisely what had been going through his head. Gullible dupe who has no experience of life, or of men, and gets taken in by the first clever conman who comes along and plays upon her insecurities. He had seen her as pathetic. She was convinced of it and she had looked at herself through his eyes with humiliation.

But, she now thought, didn't every cloud have a silver lining? She thought of Grant Adams, and of that glimpse of suffocating charm that had flashed across his face. If there was one thing that Brian had done for her, it was to make her immune to men like Grant Adams.

Even before Brian, she had always been a self-contained person. Now she guarded herself and her emotions with rigid control. She might have been a fool once, but lessons were there to be learnt from. She would never be a fool again.

It was late the following morning before she woke up, after the sort of restless night that came from sleeping in different surroundings.

It was warm in the room, but as she drew back the curtains she could see the cold outside clutching at the trees and buildings.

Emily burst into the room as she was preparing to get dressed, and Roberta said automatically, 'There's such a thing as knocking.'

Emily's long black hair had been dragged away from her face and was hanging down her back in a pony-tail, but her face still wore that suspicious, defensive expression.

'You work here,' Emily replied. 'Why do I need to knock?'

'I wish I could follow that argument,' Roberta replied, vanishing into the en suite bathroom to wash her face and then reappearing to apply some light make-up at the dressing table.

'Anyway, you should have been up hours ago.'

'Should I?' she asked drily. 'If I had known that you were that eager for my company, I would have set my alarm clock.'

'Ha, ha.'

'Actually, I got to bed quite late last night. I met your father and we remained chatting for a while.' Chatting, she thought with a silent laugh. What a way to describe that explosive encounter between them.

'You mean he came home?' Emily's voice expressed a cynicism that sounded out of place in someone that young. 'Before midnight? How good of him. Normally we cross each other in passing. He's always on the way out somewhere.'

There was a wealth of bitterness in her voice and Roberta looked at her with surprise.

'Shocked?' Emily asked. 'You wouldn't be if you knew him. I suppose you fell for all that laid-on charm, did you? He seems to have a talent with women, not that I can understand why.'

'That's a bit unfair.' Roberta shrugged herself into some clothes, making sure that she had enough under-layers to protect her from the weather outside. 'And in answer to your question, no, I didn't fall for all that laid-on charm.' Not, she thought, that he had used any on her anyway, but she wasn't going to say that.

Emily was staring at her suspiciously, as though ready to argue the point, but Roberta wasn't having it. She switched the subject skilfully away from Grant Adams, and on to the infinitely safer topic of Toronto and what there was to see.

By the end of a very tiring day, they were at least on speaking terms, even though it was a case of treading carefully in order to avoid initiating one of Emily's sulks. Roberta had discovered quite quickly that Emily was adept at them, although they would last only a short while, to be replaced usually by a battery of forthright questions which left Roberta feeling exhausted.

'I thought I was direct,' she said, as they relaxed later that afternoon in the kitchen in front of a cup of coffee, 'but you're leagues ahead of me.'

That extracted a grin from Emily, which vanished almost as soon as it had formed. 'I can see why you didn't go for Dad,' she said. 'He's not into direct women. He likes them coy and brainless.'

'Do I really?'

'They both turned at the sound of his voice. Emily with surprise, and Roberta with an expression of amusement at his daughter's reaction.

He walked into the kitchen, slinging his coat carelessly on to the counter and sitting down opposite them.

Roberta looked at him with detachment, thinking that he really was remarkably attractive. Last night she had been too caught up in her emotional reaction to his behaviour to have really examined him, but she could see now that he was the sort of man who had probably spent a lifetime turning heads. And, she thought, agreeing with Emily, spending his time playing with coy, brainless women. He had a lean, arrogant hardness about him that no doubt attracted hordes of them. She smiled, and he said in a cool voice, 'What's the joke?'

'Joke?' She threw him an unreadable look. 'I was just thinking, that's all.'

'About Toronto? Or about the brainless women that I go for, according to my daughter?

Emily was looking between them.

'What are you doing home so early, anyway?' she asked, her mouth downturned as she stared at him, and he frowned.

'I thought you might have been pleased to see me.' There was impatience in his voice.

'Why? You think showing up at a reasonable hour now and again helps to remind me what you look like?'

Grant frowned heavily. 'I don't think that remark is called for, young lady, and——'

'And what?' she muttered mutinously. 'Are you going to pack me off to bed for punishment? Or tell me that I can't have any pocket money?' She sniggered, happily oblivious to the flush of anger that had darkened his cheeks.

'We had a lovely day,' Roberta said, suspecting that if she didn't interrupt soon she would be witnessing an almighty clash.

Grant ignored her completely. He was staring at his daughter and she was staring back at him, her green eyes angry and defensive.

'When are you going to realise, young lady, that being rude isn't charming or endearing, it's just aggravating and rubs people up the wrong way.'

Emily stood up, her face flushed. 'You should know all about that!' she shouted. 'You specialise in it!' With that she ran out of the room, and Roberta looked towards the door worriedly. She didn't have a great deal of experience in dealing with adolescents, but she did know that Emily would probably lock herself in her bedroom and burst into tears.

She stood up to follow and Grant said tightly, 'Sit down.'

'But——' she began, and he cut into her with a hard voice.

'I said sit down! I didn't come back here at this hour to be subjected to my daughter's ill manners.'

Roberta sat back down and glared at him. 'What did you expect? You hardly spend any time with her. You can't think that the odd early return from work is going to fill her with delight.'

'And I don't need you to start preaching to me again,' he muttered, pouring himself a cup of coffee. 'She'll calm down. What did you two do today, then?'

'We went to the Eaton Centre and browsed around. And how do you know that she'll calm down? I think you ought to go to her bedroom and talk to her.'

'And I think you ought to stop playing at being an amateur shrink. When I need advice, I'll consult a professional.'

Roberta looked at him, bristling, and he said with lazy amusement, 'You're wearing that school-ma'am look again.'

'Because I don't happen to agree with how you react with your daughter?' she burst out.

Grant's mouth tightened into a forbidding line. 'I didn't employ you to voice opinions. I employed you to make sure Emily behaves herself in my mother's absence.'

'The two go hand in hand.' She gave him a conciliatory smile. 'She's unhappy, can't you see that? She's suffered not having a mother-figure. I'm sure most children do——'

He slammed his coffee-cup on to the table and the liquid spilled over the rim, leaving a wet patch. 'She damn well doesn't need a mother-figure!' he ground out. 'She's already had a mother-figure, enough to last her a lifetime.'

Roberta's eyes widened at his tone of voice. She had touched on a raw nerve here. Her mind flashed back to his reaction to her when he had spotted her physical resemblance to his wife. Was that why he filled his time with women? Because no one could ever live up to the woman he had married and loved?

What had she been like? She bit back the compulsive desire to ask, knowing that that would definitely cause a major explosion.

'And I hope you're not entertaining any thoughts of putting yourself in that position,' he said tersely.

She looked at him with bewilderment. 'What are you talking about?'

'Don't give me that innocent stare. You already know that my wife and you share certain physical attributes, even if they are only superficial——'

The gist of what he was saying became patently clear and Roberta felt a rush of blood to her head. 'You may think so!' she snapped. 'Emily has made no mention of any similarity!'

'Emily rarely notices anyone but herself. Subconsciously, I'm sure she's drawn the inevitable comparisons. All I'm saying is that I hope you don't intend to exploit that fact. I hope you don't let it slip your mind that you're an au pair and not a prospective mother-figure for her.'

'Is that a warning?'

'It's a piece of advice. You may have come here in good faith, but now that you know the situation there's nothing to stop you from manipulating it to your own advantage.'

'Nothing except a few principles,' Roberta informed him coldly. She could have laughed aloud at his train of thought if she wasn't so damned angry at his assumption. Involvement with a man? Good grief! She had had enough of the male sex to last her a lifetime.

'Principles can become very elusive when there's financial gain in the offing,' he said with infuriating calm. 'I've seen it in action and, believe me, it's not a pretty sight.'

'Well, you can rest assured that I have no intention of doing any such thing,' she said briefly, thankful that the hot emotion which he seemed to arouse in her had not deprived her of her power of speech. 'I'm not after your bank balance. In fact, I don't find you or your money the slightest bit appealing.'

Her words seemed to echo in the kitchen, and she could have kicked herself. She didn't want to indulge in any conversation that strayed from the strictly professional subject of his daughter with this man, yet here she was, saying the first thing that came into her head.

'Now there's an admission,' he drawled, his green eyes flickering with faint mockery. 'I was wondering what sort of man appealed to you.' The savagery had left his face completely. Now she wished heartily that it was back there because it was far easier to handle.

'Were you?' Roberta said, pink colour creeping up her cheeks. Her power of speech didn't seem nearly so reliable now. In fact, she was totally lost for words as he looked at her curiously.

'I was,' he murmured softly, 'so why don't you tell me? Not afraid, are you?'

'Of course not!' Roberta denied with a vigour she was far from feeling.

'Then please fill me in. I'm interested.' He leaned back in the chair, his hands clasped behind his head, and continued to survey her through narrowed eyes.

At this point, she thought, I should have some freezing retort on my lips. But nothing came to mind. All she could see was his overwhelming sexiness. The silence stretched around them until she was suffocating in it. Finally she gathered her wits and said with composure, 'I don't like men who are smooth and charming.'

A picture of Brian flashed into her head, and she found herself describing him in minute detail. She was hardly conscious of the edge of jaded disillusionment that had crept into her voice.

'And are you going to tell me who he was?'

Grant's question caught her by surprise and she stared at him and blinked. Everything settled back into perspective, and she recalled with horror what she had told him. She had not mentioned names, but she had nevertheless found herself imparting personal information without even realising it. Either she had suffered some bout of temporary insanity, or else he was more adept at listening than she had given him credit for.

'No one,' she said, standing up, furious with herself for dropping her defences. 'I was generalising.'

'Were you?' His eyebrows shot up in disbelief and she had an urge to throw her coffee in his face.

'If you don't mind,' she said, ignoring his question and shifting her eyes away from the mesmeric lines of his face, 'I think I'll head upstairs now and check on Emily. It's been a long day. I want to have a bath before dinner.' Her voice faded into the silence, and she pursed her lips tightly.

'Of course,' he said, not pursuing the topic. 'Toronto can be exhausting. Particularly the Eaton Centre. A marvellous place to shop, so I hear, but very tiring on the legs.'

'Isn't it?' Roberta replied politely. She wanted to get away now. As soon as his attention was off her, as he reached to pour himself another cup of coffee, she quietly slipped out of the kitchen, her face thoughtful as she headed towards Emily's bedroom.

She had made a mistake bracketing him with Brian, she decided. There really was no comparison. Brian's charm was all superficial. She could see that now, and quite probably she would have seen that at the time, had she not been so wrapped up in her own personal misery.

But Grant Adams... She frowned. He was a different cup of tea altogether. He possessed that rare, innate ability to get people to talk, to make them respond to his magnetism, and she knew that she was a novelty to him.

There was no doubt that women were attracted to him in droves, and there was also no doubt that men who could get what they wanted frequently pursued the things that were inaccessible.

He might warn her off, but there lurked a niggling thought at the back of her mind. What if, despite everything he had said, her resemblance to his wife succeeded in whetting his appetite?

You're being over-imaginative, she thought with a little laugh. Playing amateur shrink, as he had put it. It was a game she would do well to refrain from.

Emily was lying on her bed when Roberta entered, her eyes red. She immediately sat up and scowled.

'Who asked you here?' she snapped, and Roberta sat on the edge of the bed with a little shrug. 'Did he ask you to follow me up here?'

'No,' Roberta replied truthfully.

'Then why have you come?'

'To see how you were, of course. I know that you were upset, but——'

'I wasn't upset,' Emily denied, pushing her hair out of her face. 'I was annoyed. How can he carry on about me when he's the same? He's rude, arrogant...' She spluttered speechlessly and her ferocious scowl deepened.

'You are quite similar, now that you mention it,' Roberta agreed drily. 'Does he sulk as well?'

'I never sulk.' Emily's lips twitched in the glimmer of a smile. 'I react to situations.'

Roberta laughed aloud at that one. 'You're made to be a politician with statements like that,' she said with a grin, and Emily relaxed.

'I picked it up from him,' she stated. 'He always becomes evasive when he doesn't want to talk about something. For instance, did he admit to you that he went with brainless beauty models?'

Roberta shook her head. 'Why should he? It's none of my business.'

Emily propped herself on her elbows and surveyed her thoughtfully. 'I can't stand them,' she confided, sliding a sidelong glance at Roberta, 'they're awful. They giggle too much and half the time pretend to be fascinated by everything he says.'

'Maybe they are.'

'Maybe.' She shrugged nonchalantly. 'I can't see why, though—nothing he ever says to me is fascinating. No, they're just interested in netting him. You can see it written all over their faces. It's laughable really.'

'Law of averages says that one day one of them will succeed,' Roberta said lightly.

'Not if Grandmother has her way. She finds them as dislikeable as I do.'

'It's understandable that you view it like that,' Roberta said, and then she grinned. 'Lord, here I go again, trying to analyse.'

'And wrong, too. I have no objections to a stepmother, just so long as it's someone who doesn't simper.'

'What are we going to do tomorrow?' Roberta asked, not liking the sly look that was being directed at her.

'You don't simper,' Emily said. 'In fact, you don't seem at all impressed by all this.' She waved her hand grandly around the room.

'I'm not,' Roberta said hurriedly, uneasy at this turn in the conversation. 'Nor am I looking for a mate, if that's what this little conversation is leading to.'

Emily's green eyes widened in innocent shock. 'Oh, no, of course not! I never said you were. All I'm saying is that it's nice to meet someone who has their feet firmly planted on the ground. Are all English people like that?'

'All the ones I've met.' She stood up and smiled. 'Now, get freshened up. Your eyes are red. Anyone would think that you had been crying.'

At that, Emily sprang out of the bed. 'Crying? At something my father says?' she shrieked in horror. 'Never!'

But, as Roberta closed the door behind her, she could hear the tap running profusely, and she sighed.

What a situation. No wonder she had not spared any thought for her own problems ever since she had arrived. She didn't have the time. She was too busy trying to cope with everyone else's.

She unhurriedly got dressed for dinner. There was no leeway with the evening meal. Mrs Thornson made that clear. Dinner was served at seven-thirty because she had to leave very soon after that.

She was heading for the dining-room when Grant appeared from the direction of the study, impeccably dressed in a dark-coloured suit.

'Have a good evening,' he said, and she nodded. She had expected that he would be dining with them, something that she had not been particularly looking forward to, so she couldn't account for the swift feeling of disappointment that flooded through her.

Where was he off to? Did she really need to ask?

She didn't have to, because just then the doorbell sounded and he unhurriedly made his way towards it.

Roberta automatically hovered to see who would enter, her mouth going dry as a tall blonde entered the hallway. Her hair was long—waist-length—and falling turbulently around the camel-coloured coat draped across her shoulders.

She glanced towards Roberta, her exquisite features hardly registering any reaction. The glance was part of a brief sweep before her deep navy eyes settled lingeringly on Grant.

'Ready?' she asked in a throaty voice, and he nodded, sparing Roberta a backwards glance.

'See you later. And make sure that Emily gets to bed at a reasonable hour, would you?'

'Of course.' Roberta resisted the urge to salute, not that he would have seen anyway. He had already been halfway out of the door when he had addressed her.

So that's one of his brainless beauty queens, she thought. And I fancied that I would have to be careful with him.

She laughed scornfully at herself. You'll have to put a brake on that imagination of yours, my girl—it could get quite out of control.

CHAPTER THREE

IT WAS surprising how quickly you became accustomed to different surroundings.

After five days, Roberta could almost feel her body acclimatising to the intense cold, or maybe she had simply become more adept at protecting herself from it. And London seemed several light years away.

Had she really wasted all that time torturing herself over her abortive relationship with Brian? She must have been mad. Mad to have been conned out of her money in the first place, and mad to have then proceeded to spend her hours agonising over her stupidity.

From where she was standing now, it seemed positively easy to be philosophical about the whole mess.

Her relationship with Emily was still unpredictable, but getting better. The bouts of sulking were becoming less frequent, and conversation was proving less of an enormous effort than she had originally thought it was going to be.

There was still a lurking suspicion that one hesitant step forwards might be rapidly followed by two very decisive ones backwards, but Roberta was beginning to discover how to handle that situation.

It really wasn't difficult. As soon as you remembered that Emily was insecure rather than headstrong and defensive rather than aggressive, then it was fairly easy to go from there.

And the sheer joy of exploring Toronto in the company of someone who knew it intimately was enough for Roberta to put up with anything.

'But I've seen all this stuff before,' Emily had objected at the start. Roberta had been inflexible.

'I haven't,' she had stated firmly, 'and we're going to explore this city if I have to drag you kicking and screaming.'

'Some attitude from an au pair,' Emily had grumbled ill-humouredly, but she had allowed herself to be led, and had gradually taken over the reins of tour guide.

They braved the cold to travel the city centre in the streetcars, and when the cold became unbearable, they ducked into any one of the massive shopping malls to recuperate in front of cups of coffee and doughnuts.

Roberta browsed in the shops with Emily, smilingly refusing to be talked into buying anything.

'Why are you so tight with your money?' Emily asked, as they strolled through one of the department stores. She was still young enough, despite her attempts at adult behaviour, to get away with the most appallingly direct questions.

Roberta shrugged. 'I haven't got a great deal of it,' she confessed. 'Not everyone is blessed with a limitless source of funds,' she added drily, smiling when Emily's face contorted into a sardonic grimace.

'Blessed? Ha! Dad lavishes material things on me because it eases his conscience.'

'You mean because he spends so much time at work?' Roberta asked absent-mindedly, fingering the soft wool of a cashmere coat which cost the earth.

'At work and at play,' Emily replied darkly. 'You saw the type of woman he goes out with and, believe me, she's one in a long line of them.'

Roberta hurriedly changed the subject. She preferred not to talk about Grant Adams. It made her uncomfortable—she could already feel herself getting hot under the collar at the thought of him. Talk about double standards. How could he possibly expect his daughter to be well-behaved and old-fashioned, without a wayward streak in her body, when the only example of behaviour set before her was in the shape of him?

There I go again, she thought wryly, getting all het up thinking about him. It was just so damned frustrating. She resented the way he had the power to stimulate in her a host of emotions which she had always been quite successful at submerging.

Not even Brian had had that effect on her. Which, she now thought, strolling away from the cashmere coat in case Emily produced another quip about her stinginess, just went to show how much she disliked the man.

Her feet were killing her by the time they made it back to the house. Shopping in a mall in Toronto, she had decided several days ago, was similar to walking ten times around Hyde Park. Except infinitely more lethal on the bank balance and, in weather like this, far more comfortable, which made it even worse.

To cope with the cold, shopping was an enclosed affair. A vast quantity of shops, all under one roof and, she had soon discovered, all linked by the underground system.

Now, as she eased her weary feet out of her boots and lay back on the bed, she decided that bankruptcy could be very easy to achieve. A cashmere coat here, a pair of trousers there, some bits and pieces of underwear, and before you knew it you were on the quick road downhill.

There was a knock on her door and, without getting up from the bed, she yelled, 'Come on in,' only sitting up abruptly when she realised that it wasn't Emily or Mrs Thornson, but Grant.

'Hello,' she said, shifting off the bed and on to one of the chairs in the room.

He leaned against the door-frame and looked at her. 'Hard day?' he asked.

Roberta nodded, wondering what he was doing in her bedroom and wishing he would clear off. Something about that tall, lean frame sent prickles through her. 'Yesterday we went to the harbourfront, and today we went to some of the malls.' She paused. 'I feel as though I've left my legs behind somewhere. I'm only now beginning to realise how unfit I am.'

He moved across to the window and she followed his movements, noticing how gracefully he moved for someone so powerfully built. He had clearly just returned from work, was still in his suit, and she thought, another early day? What was the significance of this one? She had seen nothing at all of him recently, ever since his leggy date had shown up at the house, and she was beginning to believe Emily when she had said that her father played as hard as he worked.

Men, she thought acidly—weren't they all the same? Out to enjoy themselves, whatever the cost? And looking at him now, framed by the window, the bedroom light throwing the sharp contours of his face into relief, she told herself that he was a typical male, but more so. He had limitless women at his disposal, and he took every advantage to exploit that fact. How long had Miss Legs of the Year been on the scene? she wondered. A few weeks? Maybe longer? Only to be discarded when another model took his fancy? She decided that she heartily disapproved of him, and right now she particularly disapproved of him standing there by the window without showing any signs of leaving.

'Don't you exercise?' he asked, raising one eyebrow.

'Have you come to make polite chit-chat?' Roberta asked. 'If so, I'll be down in a minute.'

'You certainly know how to get to the point, don't you?' he said drily, not budging.

'I just think that this isn't exactly a suitable place to conduct a conversation.'

There was the faintest glimmer of amusement in his eyes as he looked at her, and she flushed.

'Emily seems to have taken to you,' he commented. 'I've just come from chatting with her, and she tells me that you're all right, she supposes, which is tantamount to a eulogy.'

Roberta smiled. 'She can be charming when she forgets that rebellious image she's trying to cultivate.'

'You'll have to let me in on your secret,' he drawled, but there was enough of a hint of seriousness in his voice to make her look at him sharply.

'No secret,' Roberta responded lightly. 'I just take time with her. If she throws a sulk, I let her, but I don't let it affect me. It's difficult to be constantly ill-mannered to someone when they don't respond.'

'You think I don't handle her correctly, then.'

'I never said that.' She stood up pointedly and walked towards the door, hovering once she had reached it.

'You seem to have mastered the art of not saying anything, but nevertheless making your meaning perfectly clear. I suppose you disapprove of my lifestyle, and I'm sure Emily hasn't been backward in supporting that.'

Roberta stared at him, unsure whether he expected an answer to that one.

'She doesn't mention it, really,' she hedged, feeling quite awkward now that she had got to her feet, but had found herself unable to actually leave the room.

'I don't believe that for a minute,' Grant remarked lazily. 'The child barely utters two words to me, but she makes herself perfectly clear on the subject of my women.'

Roberta didn't say anything. Suddenly the room was feeling very small, and images of Grant with his women flashed through her head with such graphic detail that she was alarmed. Why was it that whenever she was in his presence, it was always so damned hard to draw the line between her professional status and her private one? Much as she disliked it, he made her conscious of the fact that she was a woman.

'I wouldn't know about that,' she murmured vaguely.

'Wouldn't you?' He strolled across to where she was standing, and as he looked down at her she realised that the room was feeling much smaller now. In fact, it was difficult to breathe evenly.

'I think we ought to go down for dinner,' she said as firmly as she could. 'Mrs Thornson gets quite upset if we don't eat on time. She likes to get away at a reasonable hour, especially as she has to use public transport to get back to her house. She says that winter's a dreadful time to be standing in a bus shelter waiting for a bus.'

'Perhaps I should get her a car.'

'Wouldn't it be cheaper just to make sure you eat dinner on time?'

Those amazing green eyes were pinning her against the wall. She felt very much like a helpless moth fluttering too close to an open flame. It wasn't a very pleasant feeling. Remember, she told herself, what happened the last time you got too close to an open flame.

'I make money,' he said coolly. 'But once it's made, I don't count it.'

'Lucky old you. How nice to be in that position.'

'I don't suppose as an au pair that you are,' he said speculatively. 'Is that why you took this job? Because it was well paid?'

Roberta shrugged uncomfortably. 'Among other things.'

'What other things?'

'If you'll excuse me,' she said decisively, 'I'm going downstairs now. I don't relish the thought of Mrs Thornson's anger if she's kept waiting around.'

She turned to go, and his hand closed over her wrist. 'Wait just a minute. Forget about Mrs Thornson. You won't be having dinner here tonight. You'll be having dinner with me.'

'Is that an order?' Roberta asked after a while. 'I wasn't told that having dinner with the boss was to be part of my duties.'

Her reply had irritated him. She could see it in the fleeting change of expression on his face, but she didn't give a damn. She had meant every word that she had said. Why should she have to cope with a man who was so self-confident that he assumed everyone, including her, was somehow programmed to follow his commands?

At the back of her mind, there hovered another uneasy thought. Dinner with him spelt the sort of dangerous intimacy which she had no intention of succumbing to. She wanted to be in total control of her life from here on in. Why jeopardise that by accepting an invitation to dinner with Grant Adams? He was too damned attractive for his own good, too damned sure of himself. She thought again of Brian, of the pain and humiliation that had arisen from that terrible entanglement, and she had a sudden panicky desire to run.

'Why the hell are you so prickly?' he asked, with a note of impatient ill-humour in his voice, and she forced herself to smile.

'Was I? I'm so sorry. I was merely being honest.'

'I didn't ask for your honesty, and I'm certainly not asking you out to dinner. I'm telling you that's what you'll be doing. If you choose to think of it as an order, then by all means do so. After all, I pay your salary at the end of the day. And, before you start giving me one of those tight-lipped, prim little glares that you specialise in, I'll set your mind at rest. There won't just be the two of us. I have an important dinner engagement with a client, and I have to take someone along.'

'Then I suggest you take the blonde who turned up here the other evening.'

'Vanessa?' His mouth twisted expressively. 'No, she wouldn't do at all, much as she would relish the prospect. This is an important client. I need someone less flamboyant.'

That hurt. Less flamboyant, indeed. Well, she didn't need an interpreter to tell her what he meant. She was the sort of ordinary girl who wouldn't attract much attention. She wasn't like the statuesque Vanessa, or his exciting wife from the story the portrait had told her, or probably like any of his other women. She was attractive enough in a girl-next-door way, but not so attractive that she hogged the attention.

Was that how Brian had seen her? As presenting just the right degree of ordinariness that would make her fall for his cheap, well-used charm?

'Thank you for that little bit of honesty,' Roberta said coldly.

'I take it you'll come.' It wasn't a question, it was a statement of fact, and she looked at him with dislike.

'Do I have a choice? As you said, you do pay my salary.'

He gave her a curt nod. 'Can you be ready in half an hour? You're not one of these women who spends hours getting dressed, are you?'

'Do I look like that sort of woman?' She hadn't expected an answer, but he stared at her assessingly, his eyes roving over her body with the expert appraisal of someone well used to the female form and probably far more in tune with style than she was. They finally returned to her face, which was burning in angry embarrassment.

'No, I don't think you do,' he said smoothly. His answer didn't surprise her, but she felt that same sharp hurt that she had earlier on, and she composed her features into a deliberately cool, controlled smile.

'I'll meet you in the hall, then,' she informed him. He hesitated, as if it were on the tip of his tongue to say something else, but whatever it was it didn't materialise into words. Instead, he gave her another quick, speculative look and was gone, his footsteps muffled by the thick carpet.

Roberta closed and locked the door, just in case he got it into his head to reappear with some other unwanted titbit of honesty, and went across to her wardrobe, rapidly scanning her array of unadventurous clothing.

Not for the first time, it struck her exactly how lacking she was in those little black numbers that most women possessed in ample supply.

She was not vain and had never been terribly interested in clothes. Some of her friends spent a fortune on attiring themselves in the latest designer wear, but she had always stoutly refused to be swayed into their fervour for spending sprees.

She had spent all her life having to watch what she spent, saving for the little luxuries which she treasured but, more frequently than not, spending her money on her mother.

She sighed wearily at the selection facing her and said in a loud voice, 'You could at least look more enticing.'

In the end she chose the most passable of her dresses, a long-sleeved jade-green dress that fell to her calves in soft swirls, and after a quick shower stuck it on, with her black high-heeled shoes which had so far not been worn.

When she was finished, she looked critically at her reflection in the mirror, and an unwelcome thought popped into her head. What would Vanessa have looked like? Vampish, no doubt, in something very costly and very skimpy. Roberta had got the impression that she was a woman who liked to show the world that God had given her a spectacular figure.

Grant was waiting for her in the hall, his back to her, and she stopped for a second on the staircase to observe him at leisure. The black suit fitted him like a glove, emphasising the width of his shoulders and the leanness of his body. It wasn't fair, she thought, that one man should be blessed with such physical perfection, and that he should be so casually aware of it.

He turned towards her, not saying anything except, 'Ready?'

Roberta nodded, slinging on her black coat which had seen her loyally through more winters in England than she could remember, but which was hardly the height of high fashion.

'I decided to leave the cashmere one on the hanger in the department store,' she told him, forestalling any remarks that might have been coming her way.

'Why?' he asked, guiding her by the elbow towards his car, which was parked in the drive.

'I didn't think the colour suited me.'

He gave a low laugh. 'Maybe I should come along with you and judge for myself.'

'Maybe not,' she replied, slipping into the passenger seat. He was only joking, but what an appalling thought. Parading in front of him in a coat, twirling from side to side like some bubble-brained model, while he scrutinised her with that derisory smile on his lips, before agreeing that perhaps she was right, the colour didn't suit her after all. No thanks.

'Where are we going?' Roberta asked, as the car slid noiselessly out of the drive.

'A new place that's just opened near the harbour front. It specialises in fish.' He shot her a sidelong glance. 'You do like fish, don't you?' he asked, and she nodded.

'And what sort of impression am I supposed to give?' she questioned sweetly. 'Background and docile? Interested and intelligent?'

'Do I detect a trace of sarcasm in your voice?'

She looked at his sharp profile, then dropped her eyes to his long fingers, clasped lightly on the steering wheel.

'Of course not. I would just like to be forewarned. After all, I wouldn't want you to be embarrassed and have you thinking that Vanessa might have been better value.'

She was irritated to hear herself sounding piqued, and turned to stare vacantly out of the window.

'If I didn't know better,' he drawled, 'I might have thought that you had been bitten by the little green monster.'

'You'd be wrong, then, wouldn't you?' she responded with equanimity.

'Would I?' He threw her another sidelong look. 'You present such a discreet, business-like image to the world; maybe you inwardly aspire to the likes of Vanessa.'

That, Roberta decided, didn't merit an answer, so she remained silent.

'You strike me as the sort of girl who's always been very cautious, very careful. Am I right?'

'I don't wear miniskirts and frequent nightclubs,' Roberta replied icily, which only succeeded in bringing a slight mocking smile to his lips.

'But haven't you ever wanted to? I'm interested.'

She clicked her tongue with exaggerated impatience. Couldn't he see that she didn't want to be subject to his brand of idle curiosity? No, she thought sourly, he's probably well aware of that, but it just doesn't stand in his way.

He was persistent. If he wanted to know something, then he persevered until the mystery had been unravelled to his satisfaction. There was something vaguely disturbing about that. He was a man who controlled situations rather than the other way around, and that unnerved her.

'As a matter of fact, no,' she replied into the waiting silence. He didn't say anything. 'My father died when I was young,' she found herself explaining, 'and I guess I ended up being shaped by my environment. My mother was a very gentle woman. It never occurred to me to indulge in a wild life, because I always knew that that would have hurt her.'

'You talk in the past tense,' Grant said, his voice free of any undertone. 'Is she dead?'

'She died several months ago,' Roberta said abruptly.

'It must have been very upsetting for you.'

'Yes. It was. I don't think I shall ever fully recover. I've heard it said that the death of a loved one is a bit like losing a limb. You might accept it after a while, but you never stop feeling its absence.' It was the first time she had been so articulate in the expression of her grief with anyone and she felt a sudden and overwhelming surge of warmth for the man sitting next to her, which she stifled quickly, confused by the emotion.

'I guess you must understand that,' she said in her normal voice. 'You must have gone through the same thing yourself when your wife died.'

His face hardened imperceptibly. 'Perhaps,' he said, and she realised that he didn't want to discuss it. For some reason his wife was a taboo subject, and she changed the topic, unwilling to lose the atmosphere of mutual understanding that had suddenly developed between them.

He began telling her about his client, indirectly answering her earlier question of what attitude she should adopt.

'He's Japanese,' Grant told her. 'Very charming. Married with two children. His wife will be there as well, and she's delightful. I can't imagine you being loud and raucous, but I might as well warn you that that sort of behaviour would meet with heavy disapproval and, for reasons I won't bore you with, it's imperative that Mr Ishikomo is left with a favourable impression.'

'Is that why you didn't want to bring Vanessa?' Roberta asked. 'Because she might have become loud and raucous?'

They had stopped now, the car neatly and efficiently slotted into one of the few vacant spaces, and he turned to look at her, the shadows lending his face an air of arrogant masculinity that made her shiver.

'No,' he surprised her by saying.

'Then why? Or is that,' she added, when no reply was forthcoming, 'a hands-off subject?' She looked at him and added with veiled irony, 'I'm interested.'

'If you must know, I don't want to take Vanessa along because that might start giving her ideas. She's already started making coy references to our future together, despite the fact that I've told her often enough that I'm not the marrying kind. I've done that once and I have no intention of doing it again. No, she would just love to come along tonight and play the perfect hostess, but I can't see the point of lulling her into a false sense of security.'

'She's good enough to sleep with, but not good enough to feature as anything more meaningful in your life? Is that it?' Roberta looked at him blandly.

'I'm a man,' he replied roughly, as though annoyed by her reaction. 'I haven't remained celibate since the death of my wife. But that doesn't mean to say that I'm on the look-out for a prospective marriage partner.'

'Your wife must have meant a great deal to you.'

'She certainly made her mark on my life, yes,' he agreed, his expression giving nothing away. 'Now has that satisfied your curiosity?'

It hadn't. In fact, it had done just the opposite. It had whetted it.

'Was that why you reacted so strongly when you first saw me?' she persisted, deciding that tenacity didn't have to be limited to one of them. 'Because I brought back painful memories of her?'

'I was stupid,' Grant said flatly, pulling down his door handle and leaving her in no doubt that as far as he was concerned the matter was terminated. He paused before stepping out of the car and said over his shoulder, 'Yes, you physically reminded me of her. She had straight hair when I first met her, about your length. That's probably why Emily didn't associate you with her at all. Now, are you ready?'

She nodded, realising that he had no intention of answering anything that he wanted to keep to himself. He was throwing her a few crumbs of himself, but the rest was for his eyes only, and she doubted he was a man who could be persuaded into revealing anything, however minute, that it didn't suit him to reveal.

It didn't bother her anyway, she decided. She was curious about him because she worked for him, was in contact with his daughter every day, and curiosity was bound to rear its head. It was human nature. She had always been curious about her employers, wondered what motivated them.

Nevertheless, as they entered the restaurant, she kept giving him surreptitious looks from under her lashes. He was an enigma. A complicated jigsaw puzzle, the secret of which could elude even the most determined mind.

She thought about Vanessa and wondered whether the other woman had not yet realised that. From the sound of it, she was still trying to slot the pieces together. And in the meantime, Roberta thought with a twinge, having lots of fun doing it.

The restaurant was small and dimly lit, the décor nautical in flavour. Despite its lack of pretentiousness, though, the food turned out to be exquisite, and the company, as Grant had promised, was delightful.

The Japanese couple were easy to get along with. They neither raised controversial issues, nor did they expect them to arise. They chatted in fairly fluent English about any number of topics, their faces lighting up when Roberta questioned them about their children. They were fascinated by her job, and the fact that she adored children was clearly a mark in her favour.

By the time coffee had arrived, she wondered why she had ever resisted Grant's invitation to have dinner with him.

'I think they liked you,' he said drily, as they headed back to the house long after midnight. 'Maybe you should start a fan club. Emily, now my clients—who next? I wonder.'

Not you at any rate, she thought, feeling slightly deflated at that and then, just as quickly, alarmed by the uninvited reaction.

'They were nice,' she said, keeping her treacherous thoughts firmly under wraps. 'Uncomplicated.'

'I wouldn't bank on that,' he informed her mockingly. 'They have very high principles, as do a lot of the Japanese that I've met over the years. They believe in the sanctity of family life.'

'I take it they wouldn't exactly approve of your lifestyle, then,' she couldn't resist saying, and he frowned.

'I hadn't considered that, but no, I don't suppose they would. I've never broached the subject directly, but I do get the impression that casual affairs are not seen as desirable.' He laughed humourlessly. 'Shame life doesn't work that way over here.'

'Life works the way you want it to,' Roberta said.

'You show your age when you say things like that,' he returned, glancing quickly in her direction. 'Only the very young or the very stupid ever see things in black and white.'

His voice was laced with cynicism. What went on in that head of his?

They drove the rest of the way in silence. Outside, everywhere was still with cold. The odd person hurrying by wore the pained expression of someone anxious to get out of unpleasant weather. They predicted snow the following day, and in fact sporadically over the next few weeks, and Emily had told her with obvious relish, eyeing her flimsy boots with scorn, that snow in Canada was not a half-hearted affair. It came down with gusto, and in a matter of a couple of hours the city could be knee-deep in it.

As the car pulled into the driveway and Grant killed the ignition, he turned to face her and said lazily, 'Well, did you enjoy the evening that you were paid to go to?' From his tone of voice, he was still clearly irked at her remark, and a slight smile lifted the corners of her mouth.

'It was lovely. Thank you. The food was absolutely delicious. Seafood in England can sometimes be a matter of pot luck.'

'And the company?'

'Charming. As you told me it would be,' she replied honestly.

'And I suppose,' he said in an off-hand, mildly curious voice, 'it would not have been nearly so charming if it had been just the two of us? Maybe you would have expected a financial bonus to be thrown in for that kind of ordeal?'

She looked at him, and in the darkness of the car their eyes met. Her heart flipped over uncomfortably.

'Perhaps I would have,' she agreed in an equally off-hand manner. 'Shall we go in now? It's beginning to get a little chilly in the car.'

There was the very briefest of pauses, then he said, opening his car door, 'Why not? We can't have you freezing to death in the course of duty, can we? That's the problem with Toronto in winter,' he continued, before she had time to analyse his remark, 'the cold is just waiting to wrap around you.'

He moved around to her side and opened the door for her, helping her out of the car, and she felt an electric tingle through her coat, where his fingers rested on her arm.

'I don't suppose you'd care for a nightcap?' he asked, once they were inside the house.

Roberta raised her eyes to his and, with a rush of un-customary panic, decided that a nightcap with him was the very last thing she wanted.

'I don't think so,' she said, clearing her throat. 'I'm awfully tired.' She tried a light laugh which sounded high-pitched and nervous. 'I think I'll just retire to bed.'

'Of course,' he mocked, not taking his eyes off her face. 'I might have guessed that that would have been your answer. What a good little girl you are.'

His cool voice rang in her head as she quickly mounted the stairs to her bedroom, and was still reverberating when she finally lay down on the bed, ensconced underneath the starched sanctity of her quilt.

CHAPTER FOUR

IT SNOWED the following day, a few flakes to start with, but in a matter of a couple of hours it had become a steady white sheet which slowly covered the ground.

'Has your father gone to work in this?' Roberta asked Emily, staring out through the window in fascination. It hardly ever snowed in London. The cold winter weather usually manifested itself as rain or slush.

Emily came to stand next to her. 'He probably left at the crack of dawn. As usual.' Her little voice was threaded with bitterness and Roberta sighed. She might have made headway with her, but that certainly did not extend to Grant. Emily was still wrapped up in that explosive mixture of love and childish resentment towards her father.

'What will he do this evening if he can't get back home? Camp down on the office floor?'

Emily snickered. 'Oh, no. He'll make it home. His car's equipped for bad weather, like most of the cars over here, and anyway the company owns several flats in the city centre. Mostly for overseas clients, but quite often he uses one of them if he decides not to come back.'

In that case, Roberta thought, let's hope it continues like this. He had been on her mind ever since she had woken up, and she didn't want to see him. In fact, she wouldn't have been too distraught if he found himself marooned in one of those company flats for the remainder of her stay over here.

She didn't quite understand how it had happened, but he had somehow managed to edge his way into her consciousness, and the thought of seeing him day after day made her cold with apprehension.

A hostile Grant she could handle with no problems, but she knew that it wasn't that simple. He was unpredictable. He could be ruthlessly accusing one minute, mockingly amused the next. It disorientated her. Brian had, at least, been straightforward. There had been no kinks in his character. He had never let his mask slip and, if she had fallen for his practised charm, then at least she had had no one but herself to blame.

They spent the day lethargically leafing through books and playing games of Scrabble. By evening the snow had stopped falling, although it clearly had no intention of releasing its grip on the ground in a hurry. They had a very early meal so that Mrs Thornson could leave at a reasonable hour, and then retired to the lounge to watch television.

It was amazing, Roberta thought, watching the news. Reports of snow everywhere, but no mention of trains being grounded or the underground coming to a complete standstill. Over here, they knew how to cope with severe weather, expected it every year and took all the necessary precautions to ensure that it did not intrude on the day-to-day running of life.

When the doorbell sounded, Roberta glanced at Emily in surprise. 'Doesn't your father have a key?' she asked, and Emily shrugged, standing up and flexing her limbs.

'Maybe he wants to get us up,' she said. She vanished in the direction of the front door and returned a moment later with Vanessa in her wake.

Roberta stared at the other woman for a fraction of a second, then composed her features into a smile. Vanessa smiled back, but her eyes were on Emily.

'I brought you a present,' she said, and Emily glowered at her, looking very much her age.

'What for?'

Vanessa frowned briefly and an expression of irritation flitted across her lovely features. 'Because I would like to get to know you,' she said placatingly. 'Here.' She handed Emily a package which, after some reluctant unwrapping, turned out to be a flowered long-sleeved dress with a high collar. A very suitable style for a nine-year-old, but somehow Roberta could not imagine Emily in it at all.

'You came all the way here, in this weather, to give me this dress?' Emily asked in her usual blunt manner, and the question was met with another frown. This time Vanessa took less trouble in hiding her irritation. She glanced across to Roberta for support and Roberta smiled blankly. She wasn't getting involved in any of this. She certainly wasn't going to start taking sides.

'It was no bother,' Vanessa said. 'My car is a four-wheel-drive, though I have to admit I do feel a little thirsty after the trip.'

'Emily, go and fetch Vanessa—it is Vanessa, isn't it? —a . . .' she looked at the other woman with raised eyebrows ' . . . a cup of coffee? Or would you like something a little stronger?'

'Coffee would be fine,' she murmured, and Emily departed with a disgruntled scowl.

Vanessa turned to Roberta, leaning forwards in her chair, and Roberta had a sneaking suspicion that some sort of confidence was going to ensue.

'I guess you're pretty surprised to see me here,' she whispered, and Roberta shrugged.

'I suppose I would have expected you to come if Grant had been around,' she confessed after a while. 'Did you perhaps think that he had returned from work?' She was doing her utmost to persevere in her attempts at cordiality, but unwelcome images were flashing through her head, images of Vanessa's long fair limbs tangled with Grant's, her blonde hair enfolding their twisting bodies in a silken net.

'Oh, no,' Vanessa denied. She had a high, childlike voice which hardly seemed to match the experienced elegance of her face and body. Undemanding, Roberta thought uncharitably, the sort who says yes without a fight. 'I knew Grant would still be at work, as a matter of fact.' She paused, her eyes trying to draw Roberta into sisterly sympathy. 'That's why I came. I never get to see Emily. Her grandmother's always around. And I just thought that Emily is part of his life, so I really should get to know her a little better.' She glanced towards the door, and said in a low voice, 'Though she is a bit difficult, don't you think?'

'No,' Roberta said flatly.

'Well, you wouldn't, I guess.' Vanessa sat back and ran her fingers through her long hair. It was the colour of corn, turning to gold as it caught the light. 'I mean, you're accustomed to dealing with kiddies. It's your job.' There was nothing nasty in her tone of voice, but even so it made Roberta's hackles rise.

I've now been relegated to the status of starchy governess, she thought, a nonentity with nothing to offer except a bit of insight into a rebellious teenager.

Another thought followed swiftly on the heels of that one. Wasn't that how Grant saw her as well? He had said often enough that she reminded him of his battleaxe of a schoolteacher.

She didn't much care what he or his girlfriend thought of her, but it was a little niggling to realise that, as far as they both were concerned, she wasn't deserving of any fate other than to be stuck into a category. Prim little teacher. A little shadow that only came to life in Emily's presence.

She felt an almost malicious amusement watching Vanessa's futile efforts at trying to extract conversation from Emily over the course of the next hour. Questions were met with monosyllabic grunts, interspersed with the odd yawn. Emily was clearly not interested in playing the game of getting to know the girlfriend. Not that that daunted Vanessa.

As she stood to leave, Roberta had to grudgingly concede that she had persevered manfully in the face of opposition. The other woman must be intent on trapping Grant, she thought, and maybe it wasn't such a bad ploy. Persistence, after all, could often persuade even the most reluctant of men into commitment. Good luck to her, Roberta thought, with conflicting emotions which she had no intention of analysing.

'Does she really think I'm going to wear that dress?' Emily asked with a downturned mouth, as Vanessa's car throbbed into life and they shut the door behind her on the cold.

'It was a nice thought,' Roberta said automatically, meaning it. 'She wants to get to know you. There's nothing wrong in that.'

'Pah,' Emily muttered inarticulately. 'I'm going to bed.'

'Don't forget the dress in the lounge.' But Emily was already running up the stairs, taking them two by two,

her black hair swinging around her shoulders, and
Roberta sighed.

She carried her coffee-cup into the kitchen, washed
it, and then returned to the lounge for the dress. Was it
any wonder that her bitterness over her relationship with
Brian had flown out of her head the minute she had
entered this house?

She held the dress up to the light and absent-mindedly
looked at it, trying to picture it on Emily's angular frame.

'Charming,' a deep voice said behind her, 'though it
looks a little small for you.'

Roberta swung around to see Grant lounging by the
door, his hands tugging at his tie until it was undone,
then unbuttoning the top buttons on his shirt.

She stiffened, recalling with clarity those images of
Vanessa in his arms. Those lean brown hands, she
thought with pursed lips, had travelled all over the
woman's body. It was an effort to appear natural.

'It's not mine,' she said succinctly, folding it and
placing it on one of the side tables. 'It's your daughter's.'

He walked towards the bar, which was cleverly cam-
ouflaged in an old carved cabinet, and poured himself
a drink.

'Sit down,' he said irritably, 'and stop hovering there
with that worried expression on your face. I'm not about
to have you for dinner.'

Roberta sat down and continued to look at him from
under her lashes. Talk about treating people like puppets
on strings, she thought, wondering why she had obeyed
his command without question.

'I'm relieved to hear that,' she said lightly. He was in
a funny mood tonight.

He walked across to her and muttered conversationally, 'I'm sure you are.' He leant over her, sup-

porting his body on both arms of her chair, and said, with a challenging inflexion in his voice, 'Tell me, has anyone ever offered to eat you for dinner?' He gave a short laugh and turned away, prowling around the room, pouring himself another drink. 'So did the two of you venture out in this weather to do some shopping?'

Roberta breathed a sigh of relief. She didn't feel up to coping with that habit he had of trying to antagonise her into a reaction.

Far better to stick to safe topics, and what could be safer than the weather?

'We couldn't face the prospect of battling our way through that snow,' she said. 'Emily may be used to it, but I'm not.'

'So where did the charming little flowered dress come from?'

'Your girlfriend, as a matter of fact.' She lowered her eyes.

'Vanessa was over here?' Grant asked sharply, and Roberta nodded.

'What did she want?'

'To see Emily,' Roberta said innocently.

'What for?'

'Why don't you ask her?'

'I'm asking you!' He swallowed his drink and poured himself another. Then he looked at her over the rim of the glass, his green eyes glittering like two dazzling, hard jewels. 'So you can stop looking as though nothing's going on in that head of yours. After what I told you last night about not wanting her to get ideas, the least you could have done was to avert this sort of situation.'

Roberta's eyes flashed angrily, but she kept her voice under control when she spoke. 'She's your responsibility. I didn't come here to get mixed up in your private

life. I came here to look after your daughter, and that
was it!'

'That's not the song you sing when you're preaching
to me about setting a bad example,' he mocked.

'You're right,' Roberta agreed, thinking on her feet.
'You and your daughter are inextricably linked. Which
is why I happen to understand why Vanessa wants to get
to know Emily.'

'Very clever,' he said drily, appreciating the twist in
her logic. 'And what was Emily's reaction to Vanessa's
gift?'

'You should ask her yourself,' Roberta said, shrugging.

'Maybe I'll do just that. And maybe you're right as
well about Vanessa. I suppose I should be flattered. It
shows how much she must want me, don't you think?'

'There's no accounting for taste.'

'That's a rich remark coming from you,' he drawled,
moving to sit on the chair facing hers, and inspecting
her through lazy, narrowed eyes. 'After your sour relationship that made you run over here to escape, that
is a rich remark indeed.'

Roberta's eyes flew to his face. 'What are you talking
about?'

'I'm talking about that man who let you down. The
smooth-talking charmer you described in such detail to
me the other evening.'

Her face began to burn. Well, what did she expect?
He was no fool. In fact, just the opposite. He had developed shrewdness into an art form. Did she really think
that her description of Brian had gone unnoticed, even
though no name had been mentioned and she had certainly not indicated that she had been describing someone
close to her?

There was no point denying it, so she remained silent, lacing her fingers together and unlacing them, keeping her eyes away from his face.

'It must have been quite some experience for you to have flown thousands of miles across the water just to escape,' he said casually, though the green eyes on her face were intent.

'I don't want to talk about him,' Roberta muttered finally.

Grant shrugged his shoulders. 'You're entitled to your secrets,' he drawled. 'We all are.'

She stood up, ready to leave, and he said lazily, 'Aren't you going to offer to get me something to eat?'

'Would you like something to eat?' she asked stiffly, and he nodded.

'What can you cook?'

'Mrs Thornson left some casserole in the oven for you. I can do some vegetables to go with it.'

'Fine.'

She headed towards the kitchen, the hairs on the back of her neck prickling as she was aware of him following her. Was he doing this on purpose? she wondered. Did he know how uncomfortable he could make her feel? She sincerely hoped not. She preferred to let him think that she was cool and in command, even though it was an image which he found laughable. Better that, than to think... To think what? Her pulses began to race in dizzy chaos. To think, she confessed to herself, her mouth dry, to think that she was attracted to him.

Because she was, wasn't she? The thought made her body go cold. You damn fool, she told herself fiercely, what was the point of anything if you just continued to make a habit of stepping into the same stupid traps?

She switched on the microwave, and quickly and efficiently opened a can of sweetcorn, emptying the contents into a saucepan, her back to him, nervously aware that he was looking at her from where he was sitting at the kitchen table.

She felt like a rabbit unwittingly caught in a fox's lair. Just now the fox was replete, satisfied, but that didn't quell the desire to run back to the safety of an underground burrow.

She dished out his food, carefully spooning out the sweetcorn on to the plate.

She handed him the plate, and he said demurely, but with wicked amusement in his eyes, 'Thank you so very much.'

'Well…' she muttered, fidgeting and eyeing the kitchen door.

'Talk to me. I've had a hard day. I need some relaxing conversation.' He gestured towards the chair and she sat down. Lord, how she would have preferred to run, but instinct told her that running would only arouse his interested curiosity, and that was the last thing she wanted.

'Why did you bother to trudge all the way back here?' she asked, her hands folded on her lap. 'Emily told me that your company has several flats in the centre. Why didn't you stay there?'

'The pleasures of hearth and home,' he said, attacking his food with vigour. Most people had to watch what they ate. He, she thought, probably had some alien metabolism that changed food into muscle in a matter of seconds. 'Besides, the flats were in use and my car's more than capable of making the journey back here even in more severe conditions. Do you have a car in London? Do you drive?'

She nodded. 'I drive, but no, no car, I'm afraid. It's a luxury in London. The underground is quite adequate and, besides, the traffic over there is horrendous, and finding somewhere to park is even worse.'

'Do you miss it?' he asked suddenly. 'Are you homesick?' He wasn't looking at her.

'I have no relatives,' Roberta said lightly, her heart constricting as it always did whenever she thought about her mother. 'So, no, I'm not homesick at all. I like it here, in fact. It's much cleaner than London.'

'I always think that a tidy city appeals to someone with a tidy mind,' he said wryly, and she relaxed. She knew that like this, when he was at ease, was when she she should be erecting her defences most sturdily, but it was easy to forget.

'You make that sound like an insult.'

'Do I?' He smiled, one of those rare, devastating smiles that took her breath away. 'I don't mean to. There's a lot to be said for a tidy mind. Right now, mine feels decidedly cluttered.'

'Why?'

'I have some important deals going through at the moment—— '

'The Japanese one?'

'Among others,' he agreed. He had finished eating, and he took his plate to the sink, looking almost incongruous as he washed it and stacked it on to the draining-board.

'You should have returned home a bit earlier,' Roberta said, unable to resist the temptation to be snide. 'Vanessa might have relaxed you.'

'Oh, I don't know.' He turned to face her, and the expression on his face sent her pulses racing. 'You're doing quite well.'

She stood up and he moved towards her. He hadn't said anything, but he didn't have to. It was written all over his face, and the worst thing was that she couldn't move a muscle. She was hypnotised by those green, intent, vaguely amused eyes.

He stood next to her and she looked up at him, uncertain what to say to break this electric atmosphere that had suddenly sprung up between them, not knowing even whether she would be able to get the words out of her mouth.

'You look like a wild animal about to take flight,' he murmured softly. 'Why do I seem to have that effect on you?' He cupped her face with one hand, gently stroking the side of her cheek with his thumb. A simple action which he somehow managed to invest with wildly erotic meaning.

'I'm not Vanessa.' She struggled to get control of her voice.

'No, you're not, are you?' he mused, before his head swooped downwards and his mouth claimed hers.

For the briefest of moments, she returned his kiss, melting under the persuasive impact of his lips, then she pushed him away, and her hands were trembling.

'Don't!' she said sharply, stepping backwards. Reality had a way of bringing you crashing down to earth. For a while, as she had felt his body hard against hers, it had been temporarily suspended, but now she could see well enough that he was tired; he wanted her to help him unwind.

She had been used once before, she certainly had no intention of repeating the experience.

'Are you as virtuous as you'd like me to believe?' he asked, his eyes cool. He wasn't going to push her into anything, but he didn't like being rejected, she realised.

'You can believe what you like.'

'Are you still in love with this man who ditched you?' The question was so surprising that it caught her completely unawares, bringing a red stain to her cheeks.

'I wish I'd never told you about...that,' she threw at him bitterly. 'I never would have if I had thought that it would have been used in evidence against me.'

'That's not what I'm doing,' he grated impatiently, raking his fingers through his black hair.

'Isn't it?'

'You know it isn't. And you still haven't answered my question.'

'And I won't be,' Roberta said, as angry with him as with herself for allowing her guard to fall so completely, even if it was for a very short time.

'Do you know something? I've never met a woman as——'

As what? She would never know, because just then the kitchen door was pushed open and Emily stepped into the hall, immediately sensing the current running between them. How could she fail to? It was intense enough to be almost tangible.

She stared suspiciously between them. 'I've come for a glass of water,' she said, her hands on her hips, her eyes alive with curiosity. 'Am I disturbing something?'

'No!' Roberta smiled reassuringly. 'I was just about to go up to bed myself. I'll wait for you, we can go up together.'

'How touching,' Grant muttered under his breath. He looked at his daughter. 'And don't I even get some sort of greeting?'

'Oh, hello.' Emily poured herself a glass of water and drank it in one gulp.

'I've been told that Vanessa came round here to see you,' he said, not looking at Roberta at all, and Emily nodded. 'She bought you a dress,' he persevered, and that received another nod.

'She's trying to buy her way into my affections,' Emily said sourly. 'You can tell her from me that it won't work.'

Grant grinned, and for a second Emily looked almost dazzled. 'Sure,' he said, and she reluctantly grinned back.

From the sidelines, Roberta was beginning to feel slightly redundant. It was as though father and daughter had reached across the waters and briefly touched each other.

Then Emily looked at Roberta, back to her usual self. 'Ready?' she asked, and Roberta nodded.

'Goodnight,' Roberta said sweetly, quite in control now that she had managed to assert herself with him. 'I do hope the weather's a bit better tomorrow.'

'Oh, I do hope so too.' He mimicked her very English accent, and nodded in Emily's direction.

As soon as they were out of the kitchen, Emily turned to her, her eyes bright with inquisitiveness. 'What was happening in there when I came in?' she asked.

'Nothing,' Roberta murmured innocently, walking up the stairs, with Emily positively skipping by her side in childish frustration.

'It didn't look like nothing to me. Was he kissing you?' she asked, and Roberta said quickly,

'Of course not!'

'Do you fancy him?'

That, she felt, she was far more comfortable with answering. 'Your father's an attractive enough man,' she said, taking a deep breath, and wondering how she could channel the vast array of descriptions of him into a few succinct phrases, 'but he's definitely not my type. He's built for women like Vanessa.'

'I hope not,' Emily said, branching off to her own bedroom, 'because she's the last person I intend to have as a stepmother.'

Roberta let herself into the bedroom and sank heavily on to the bed.

Between Emily and Grant, she felt as though she had lost control of her life altogether. It was not a pleasant sensation. Emily she could cope with, but there was no way that she was going to let Grant put her through any tug of war, either mental or emotional.

She got up and went across to the window, staring outside at the white drifts of snow. The weather had not warmed sufficiently to instigate any kind of thaw, although the weather forecast did predict no fresh falls, at least for the time being. Not that weather forecasts could be taken as the gospel truth. She grinned to herself and thought about the last time the weather forecast had firmly denied hurricane warnings, only to have to admit their oversight with very red faces the day after.

She drew the curtains together, the ebb and flow of her thoughts preventing her from settling into sleep.

Each disturbing thought lingered just long enough for her to reach out and try to grasp it, but no sooner had she stretched out her hand than it vanished, only to give way to another, equally disturbing.

She thought about Emily, sweet and impressionable underneath her abrasive exterior. For the first time since she had started doing au pair work, she knew that she would have to be careful not to become too involved. In the past, she had always been fond of her charges, but there had never been any difficulty in moving on. Like a doctor who sympathised with his patients, but was smart enough to know where to draw the line between care and over-involvement.

But then, she thought, her charges had all been under seven years old. It was different with Emily.

And then there was Grant, more complicated than his daughter and far more dangerous.

He made no bones about concealing the sort of man he was, one who was not prepared to settle down, one, perhaps, who was still controlled by the memories of his late wife. But a man who was only too aware of his sensual appeal, and it was that awareness that made him dangerous. Self-confidence could be a heady aphrodisiac. She wouldn't let it get to her; she couldn't afford to. She had wept too many bitter tears over Brian. Tears of self-pity and shame and anger. She never wanted to weep like that again.

The jumbled thoughts sifted through her brain, giving her a headache, and when she did finally fall asleep it was into a sleep that was restless and plagued with alarming dreams.

When she woke up, the first thing she did was to wander across to her window and stare outside, where the snow was still lying in pristine splendour.

Half of her loved the sight of it, its untouched beauty. It was like looking through your window at a picture postcard. The other half was deflated at the prospect of either battling a way through it outside, or else admitting defeat yet again and remaining indoors.

Mrs Thornson had already said that she might take one week's holiday to stay at home and catch up on some decorating with her husband just while the snow lasted. At least she and Emily could busy themselves with some cooking. Even if it were just for the two of them, it would still be great fun. Roberta rather liked cooking; it was the sort of solitary pastime which she relished, and her mother had been an appreciative audience. From as far back as she could remember, her efforts had always been applauded. Unbelievable loyalty, when she thought back to some of her youthful disasters.

She got dressed unhurriedly, slipping on her jeans and a baggy jumper, sprinting down to the kitchen to make herself a cup of coffee before Emily woke up.

Emily slept with the gay abandon of the young, rarely rousing herself until at least nine o'clock, and Roberta had got into the pleasurable habit of enjoying a relaxing half-hour or so before her day really began.

She made herself her cup of coffee and headed off to the lounge to enjoy it.

When she reached the doorway, she stopped in shock, her eyes taking in Grant's figure on the sofa, his long legs stretched out in front of him, a stack of papers on the table and on the floor.

'What are you doing here?' she stammered. She had successfully managed to put all thoughts of the night before to the back of her mind, relegating his tantalising, seductive kiss to an unfortunate, not-to-be-repeated experience.

Now, seeing him here unexpectedly, the memory came flooding back as if it had all taken place only minutes before.

'What does it look like?' he rasped.

Definitely not in a good mood. His brows were meeting in an impatient frown.

'Catching up on paperwork?' Roberta asked. 'Or just appreciating the joys of indoor life?'

'The former, as you show such interest.'

She went across to one of the chairs and sat down, carefully sipping her coffee.

'I've been up all night,' he said with restless impatience, and Roberta raised her eyebrows.

'Insomnia? Perhaps you should consult your doctor about that.'

'I'm glad you find my lack of sleep amusing. I don't suppose you could channel your amusement into getting me a cup of coffee, could you?'

Roberta ignored him. 'You weren't really working all night, were you?'

He scowled. 'How very perceptive of you. I got a call around midnight, and I've had to spend the whole damn night revising some of the documents for this Japanese deal.'

'I see.' She looked at him sympathetically. 'Maybe you should get some sleep now. You must be exhausted.'

'Don't be ridiculous, woman. I can't just grab some sleep——'

'—simply because you're exhausted?'

'The work won't get done if I do, will it?' he growled, and she felt an absurd temptation to laugh.

'Sorry,' she said meekly. 'Of course it won't. Is there some kind of deadline, then?'

He looked at her as though she were terminally stupid. 'Yes, there's a deadline. If there weren't, do you really think that I would spend the night working out of a sense of fun?'

'I have no idea. Would you?'

He threw her a ferocious scowl. 'How enriched my life is with that sense of humour. Any chance of some coffee and spare me your quips?'

'Sure. Black?'

He nodded curtly, his attention back on the papers spread across his lap, and she vanished back to the kitchen, reappearing minutes later with a mug which she handed to him.

'And you might as well stick around,' he informed her bluntly. 'That deadline is a meeting the day after tomorrow.' He looked at her shrewdly, and this time a smile was on his lips. 'You did say that you could drive, didn't you?'

CHAPTER FIVE

ROBERTA looked at him cautiously. 'Yes, I did mention that in passing,' she said, not liking that smile. 'Why?'

'Because I need you to drive me somewhere,' he informed her patiently. 'Obviously. Why else would I ask?'

'Can't you take a taxi?'

'No. It's too far.'

'Too far?' Roberta repeated faintly. 'Where exactly do you want me to drive you? And why can't you drive yourself?'

'I have a house near Lake Simcoe to the north-east of here. Well, more of a cabin, really. Anyway, that's where I need to be. And I can't drive myself because I shall need to carry on working on the trip up. How can I do that if I'm driving?'

He looked at her as though that meagre explanation settled everything. It didn't, and if he thought that he could relax back in that damned sofa and assume that she had agreed to chauffeur him to some obscure part of the country, then he was in for a shock.

'Excuse me,' she said, resting her coffee-cup carefully on the table. 'If you don't mind me disturbing your concentration——'

'Of course I don't mind,' he threw at her without glancing in her direction, 'though you could make yourself slightly more useful by tidying up some of the papers on the floor for me. In numerical order.'

'I have no intention of doing any such thing,' Roberta
said, momentarily distracted, 'and please don't feed me
that line about how you pay my salary.'

'My time is money,' Grant grinned, 'and think of the
time you'll be saving me. Although,' he added, 'I do
pay your salary, now that you mention it.'

'Oh, for heaven's sake!' She knelt down and began
gathering the papers together, quickly sifting them into
order. He handed her another stack without looking up,
and she glared at his downbent head.

'Don't look so ill-humoured,' he said with a straight
face. 'Don't you like the thought of helping your fellow
man?'

Only some of them, she wanted to respond, and you
definitely don't rate on the list.

'Done,' she announced after a few minutes, dumping
them unceremoniously on the sofa next to him, and he
murmured, with barely concealed amusement,

'Good girl. What a good little secretary you'd make.'

Don't you use that languid, amused tone with me, she
wanted to wail. Instead she threw him an impotent, cold
glare and dragged her thoughts back to the matter in
hand.

'Another thing I'm not willing to do, in fact not paid
to do, is act as your chauffeur. I have no experience
driving on the right-hand side of the road.'

'You'll never learn until you try.'

'I don't want to learn,' she snapped. 'What I want to
do is enjoy a walk around the harbour front with Emily
and have a relaxing day.'

'Want, want, want. Typical woman,' he muttered,
eyeing her from under his lashes. 'Anyway, as I said,
this meeting is very important. I have to get there, one
way or another.'

'The another option sounds fine to me,' Roberta said stubbornly, but half of her already knew that she would end up driving him God knew where. He was relentless. And, right now, being charming with it. He obviously had decided on that tactic in order to win her over. How transparent, she thought.

'The meeting is the day after tomorrow at a hotel relatively close to the cabin. But I need to get to the cabin tomorrow night. I want to do some vital preparatory work there, and I have all the necessary equipment. I can take the computer disks up, feed them into my computer at the cabin and, by the time the meeting rolls round, everything will be exactly where I want it. I can easily take a taxi to the hotel and get a ride back down to Toronto.'

'How nice to see that you have it all worked out,' Roberta said with an acidity that was apparently lost on him.

'It pays to think ahead in life.'

'And where do I fit in?'

'I would have thought that that would have been obvious. You drive me up to the cabin. No need to stay, you can be back here by evening.'

'Well, that certainly is a tempting proposition,' she said sarcastically. 'In other words, you basically want me to spend the day on the road. In this weather.'

'Oh, the weather will be no problem,' Grant assured her. 'The roads will be clear. There hasn't been any more snow since that initial fall and there won't be.'

'And you've studied meteorology, have you? Or do you think it's enough that another fall of snow might ruin your plans, so ordering it not to is sufficient?'

He stared at her, his hands behind his head.

'You seem reluctant,' he said blandly, turning to face her.

'How observant,' she muttered under her breath. 'And what about Emily?'

'You'll be back by nightfall, as I said.'

'And when do we leave?'

He shot her a vaguely smug look. 'Tomorrow morning. Early. No point courting the inevitable traffic jams.'

Roberta looked at him helplessly. She didn't fancy the idea of tackling the road system for the first time in snow, and she fancied even less the prospect of being cooped up with him in a car for hours on end.

'Now,' he said, deciding for both of them that the matter had been settled, 'perhaps you would care to help me to the study with some of these papers?'

Do I have a choice? she wondered, moving over to where he was holding out some folders for her.

Their fingers touched, a brief physical contact, and the warmth shot through her like an electric current, almost making her jump back in shock.

It frightened her, this response to him. She so badly wanted to have her life back in control, to know that she would never fall foul of her common sense again.

She so desperately didn't want to have to cope with this unwanted, bewildering response to him.

They heard the front door open just as they reached the study, and Roberta breathed a sigh of relief. Mrs Thornson. At least that was something.

Emily had also roused herself at long last. Roberta could hear her flying down the stairs, feel her pause in the hallway as she took in the sight of the two of them vanishing into the study. It was no surprise when her little face appeared at the study door.

'What's the matter with you?' She directed the question ungraciously at Grant, who shot her a cautious, defensive look. 'What are you doing here?'

'I already had this conversation with your au pair,' he said. 'Work. I haven't had a wink of sleep all night. I'm functioning on sheer momentum at the moment.'

Emily gave a smirk that said, Work, what else would keep you at home? and he turned to Roberta with a grimace. 'Have you ever seen such depth of sympathy?'

'I'm sure your daughter is extremely sympathetic.' She directed the observation to Emily with a meaningful frown.

'You do look haggard,' Emily admitted, with a small, shy smile that vanished almost as soon as it appeared.

Roberta had deposited the files on the desk and stood back, as far away from him as she could reasonably get without actually leaving the room.

'I've really never seen you look so tired, Dad,' Emily said, staring at him as if he were a creature from another planet.

'You make me sound like a robot,' Grant observed drily. 'Believe me, I've been as tired as this before. I suppose you don't remember the times I've stayed up with you when you were ill. You're more responsible for the lines on my face than any amount of work.'

Emily shot him a look that was a touching mixture of defensiveness and warmth.

'Would you like me to get you anything?' she asked awkwardly after a while, and he smiled. It almost hurt Roberta to see how much he appreciated this unexpected thaw in his relationship with his daughter. It might only be temporary, but he was grateful for it. Wasn't it funny, she thought, the number of things in life that you just couldn't control, however much money or will-power you had?

He shook his head and drawled, 'No, thank you, darling. I've already had my ration of toast and coffee for the morning.' He began fiddling with the computer terminal, his fingers expertly moving over the keyboard until a series of reports flashed up on the screen.

'Lunch, however,' he said, with his back to them, 'would be nice.'

They left him absorbed in whatever was on the screen, and spent the rest of the day out in the snow. It was bitterly cold but, with no wind, quite delightful.

Emily, Roberta noticed, was rather subdued. She could guess what was going on in the child's mind. Had her father changed or had she? Either way it had been apparent that she had felt an empathy with him which she had not done in a long time, and it had left her thoughtful.

She hardly raised an argument when Roberta told her that she would be out of the house the following day.

'He's bossing you about again,' she said. 'Typical. Always giving orders and expecting them to be followed, acting as if the entire world revolves around him.' But her voice lacked its usual childish bite.

Mrs Thornson had gone by the time they returned to the house, leaving them some food and a note saying that she would see them all the following Monday as she had decided to take that week off after all.

Emily took her father a plate of food into the study, where he had been glued to his terminal since they had left the house in the morning, and Roberta stuck her head around the door a couple of hours later to find that the food had not been touched.

She picked up the plate of cold food and frowned. 'You should eat. Keep your strength up,' she said. 'You've left the lot.'

He broke off what he was doing to look at her, rubbing his eyes wearily with his fingers.

'Thank you for the concern. Actually, I didn't even notice it there,' he said. 'This damn deal is eating up my time.'

Roberta regarded him in silence. 'Can't you take a break from it for a while?'

'And what about the deadline?' he said drily. 'It isn't exactly conducive to taking time off. Where's Emily?'

'Watching television,' Roberta answered lightly. 'Some detective show. She complains about how boring it is every time it's on, but she still watches it.'

He looked away from her, and when he spoke there was a hesitation in his voice which he tried to hide under a guise of gruffness. 'She seems a little more settled,' he began.

There was silence, and Roberta smiled slightly. 'She appreciates having you at home, even if it isn't often, and even if she doesn't always show it.'

He grunted something unintelligible. That masterly self-control was, for once, missing. When it came to his daughter, Roberta realised, he was still groping about for the right solution to a perplexing problem. It was the one aspect in his life that he found himself incapable of handling with his usual clever dexterity.

'Be ready tomorrow morning,' he said briefly. 'We'll leave at six.'

'Six?'

'That way we can avoid the bulk of the traffic, and you can be back here at a reasonable hour.'

'Any more orders?' she asked, moving to the door with his plate, and he turned to her, his brilliant eyes glinting.

'None that you're likely to obey.'

Roberta flushed and hurried out of the room, closing the study door behind her.

Later, as she lay on her bed, she wondered what Grant would think if he knew just how susceptible she was to his masculinity. Would he be flattered? Amused? Embarrassed? Maybe, she thought with a flash of insight, he would see it as a ploy to get herself into his bed, to play on the love he felt for his wife by flaunting her similarity in front of him so that she could wheedle her way to his bank account. Hadn't he already warned her that it was something he would be on the look-out for?

At any rate, they were all very good reasons for making sure that he never suspected what she felt.

And, she thought, at least she recognised her own weakness. There was no point denying it and, having faced it, she decided that it might be unsettling, scary even, because of what it said about her precious self-control, but it was really no threat to her peace of mind, because to be aware of a problem was halfway to resolving it.

Brian had been a different matter. She had not faced her gullibility soon enough.

She had set her alarm-clock for five, and when it shrilled next to her the following morning she groggily dragged herself out of bed, trying not to give in to instant depression at the blackness outside or at the long drive ahead of her.

Emily, when Roberta tiptoed into the room to say goodbye, was engulfed under the duvet. Roberta shook her slightly and said, 'See you later,' getting a tired grunt for her efforts.

Grant was waiting for her in the hall.

'About time,' he greeted her, and Roberta said sweetly,

'And a very good morning to you, too.' She had felt quite sleepy as she had trudged down the stairs, but the sight of him had now banished all her drowsiness. He seemed to have that effect on her.

She glanced at him hopefully and said, 'I don't suppose you feel up to driving yourself after all?'

'Difficult,' Grant admitted. 'I've covered the bulk of the work, but I still have a few finishing touches to put to it which I can do in the car. Then, once I get to the cabin, it'll just be a matter of transferring the important sections on to the computer.' He handed her the keys to the car. 'Don't be reckless. I don't fancy ending up in hospital.'

What a paragon of politeness you are, she thought, taking the keys off him and gritting her teeth against the bone-aching cold as she opened up the car and eyed the dashboard with trepidation. It looked like the control panel of a plane. And she was supposed to get to grips with this?

It was easier than she had expected. The car was automatic, so there was no problem having to adjust to unfamiliar gears and, she conceded, it was a remarkably comfortable car to drive. Large, the seats luxuriously padded, and everything electronically controlled so that there was no fumbling about trying to get things into position.

Grant knew the route well enough not to consult a map, and gradually she began to feel more confident about the drive up.

She relaxed enough to ask him questions, her eyes briefly leaving the road now and again to appreciate the scenery, and he spoke about the terrain with love. He had the sort of deep, persuasive voice that charmed, and he sprinkled his descriptions with enough dry wit and humour to keep her amused.

As the darkness around them paled into tentative daylight, the roads become more crowded, but by then the bulk of the journey had been accomplished.

'We've covered the brunt of it,' he said, slanting a sideways look at her. 'That wasn't too bad, was it?'

Roberta didn't look at him; she was too busy peering around her, cautiously keeping a very safe distance between herself and the nearest vehicle. Accidents frequently happened through misplaced self-confidence on the road, and it was a trap that she had no intention of falling into.

'I'm not used to driving,' she confessed. 'As I said, I didn't have a car in London.'

'And your boyfriend?' The question, thrown casually at her, caught her unawares, and she replied without thinking,

'He didn't like me behind the wheel of his car. I don't think he trusted me enough with it.'

'Nice man,' Grant said mildly, and she frowned, not really able to defend Brian in any way whatsoever.

They continued for a while in silence, and she only realised that the weather had deteriorated when the first flakes of snow began to hit the windscreen.

She glanced across at Grant worriedly.

'It's snowing,' she said, stating the obvious. The windscreen wipers were now on full, and as fast as they cleared the screen it became speckled with the dusty flakes.

'We're not far away,' he answered in a clipped voice, but she was feeling distinctly alarmed by the time the car swerved off the main road and began the pains-taking manoeuvre through isolated territory towards the cabin.

She had slowed down considerably to accommodate the change in the weather, but by the time they neared the cabin the snow was so thick that she was driving almost at a crawl.

She hardly saw the place until it was looming in front of her, a small building with just the sort of rustic charm associated with hideaways near a lake.

She switched off the ignition and turned to him. 'I can't possibly get back in this,' she said, angry with him for making her drive him up here in the first place.

He nodded curtly, staring out through the window. 'We'd better get inside, and quick.'

He opened the door and ran ahead of her to unlock the cabin, while she followed quickly, head bent against the snow, her eyes disturbed and anxious.

There was a sort of terrible beauty about the way the ground was rapidly being blanketed under the snow, which was covering over their tracks even before they were inside the cabin.

'What am I going to do?' she wailed, staring at him.

'There's no point in becoming hysterical,' he pointed out, moving across to the window and inspecting the scene outside. He turned to face her. 'I'll light a fire, we might as well get some warmth in here.'

Roberta watched in silence, fighting her hysteria, while he laboriously lit the fire until it was glowing.

Keep calm, she told herself, but as soon as she thought of being cooped up here with him, the hysteria assaulted her again.

She distracted herself by looking around the cabin. It was simple, but not depressingly so. One large lounge-diner, a kitchen which seemed remarkably well kitted out and, just off the lounge, a door which no doubt led to the bedroom. The sort of place where lovers would have a field day. Had he come here with his wife? Stupid question, of course he had. This place was made for courting, but that was about it.

He had sat down on the sofa in front of the fireplace and Roberta walked across to face him, her arms folded across her chest.

'You've got me up here,' she said carefully. 'Now what are we supposed to do about this?'

'Wait it out. Do you think I'm any happier about this than you are?'

'How long is this snow likely to last?'

'Hard to say,' Grant remarked. 'A couple of days at the outset.'

'Two days?' Her voice was a shrill whisper.

'You look as though you've been condemned to a stint in hell. I won't rape you, if that's what you're afraid of.' He gave her a smile that was devoid of any humour.

'I was worried about Emily,' Roberta hedged, angry at the panic that had gripped her by the throat. 'Mrs Thornson is going to be away, and——'

'Phone her.' He waved towards the telephone. 'Or rather, bring it here. I'll talk to her.'

She brought him the phone, wandering across to the window while he explained the situation to his daughter. The thought of two days out here, stuck, was awful, overwhelming. A drive up she could manage well enough; she could fill that with polite conversation and make sure that her self-control was well and truly in place, but two days, if not more, in a cabin miles away from nowhere filled her with dismay.

'I can't stay here,' she said flatly, turning around to look at him. 'Surely I can make my way back to the main road before the snow gets too deep?'

'Don't be ridiculous. Look at the weather, woman. Do you really think that you would stand a chance if you set off now? You probably wouldn't make it as far as the bottom of the lane, and believe me I have no intention of beating a path through the snow searching for you.'

'This is all your fault!'

'There's no point dwelling on whose fault it is. The simple fact is that we're here, and there isn't the remotest chance that we can get out for the time being. You should thank your lucky stars that we managed to get here in one piece. This kind of snow can be deadly.'

'There are a lot of things in life that I could thank my lucky stars for,' Roberta muttered, angry at his tone of voice and at her lack of composure, 'and believe me, being stranded here with you isn't one of them.'

His mouth tightened. 'I don't like your tone of voice,' he said tersely.

Roberta strolled across to the fire and stared down at the leaping flames. She hadn't meant to sound antagonistic, but the thought of enforced confinement with a man, particularly this one, had made her voice sharp and querulous.

'Is this place all right for food?' she asked, making a determined effort not to lose her cool.

'Yes. I make sure that it's well stocked every time I come up here.'

'And do you come up here often?' It had been meant as an inoffensive, polite, keeping-her-cool kind of question, but as soon as it was out she realised that it could easily be misconstrued as nosiness, and she rushed on hurriedly, 'I mean, it seems rather odd to come here for a night, when your meeting isn't until tomorrow morning and in a hotel.'

Grant shrugged. 'I have a computer terminal here. The hotel which was booked doesn't run to such luxuries.'

'Why couldn't you have had your meeting in Toronto?'

'I don't suppose this will mean a great deal to you but, if you must know, this particular deal is extremely price-sensitive. Any hint of it to the outside world could jeopardise it, not to mention significantly affect my corporation's stock price.'

'Hence the secrecy.'

'In instances like this, it pays to be careful.'

'Lucky you happened to have this cabin, then.' She sat down, feeling much more in control now. He had been right, of course, panicking wouldn't get her anywhere at all. Problems assumed massive importance the more you dwelled on them.

And face it, what was she really scared of? He wasn't going to rape her, as he had so succinctly told her.

'I've had it for a number of years. It's always proved . . . useful.'

The meaning of his words echoed disturbingly in the room.

'I expect the Vanessas of this world would be most impressed with this slice of solitude,' she heard herself saying. Why was it, she thought, annoyed with herself, that she managed to come out with the most provocative remarks whenever she was in the company of this man?

She had never before in her life felt the need to explore someone else's depths. Even Brian she had accepted at face value, more fool her.

She had been quite content to skate through life without being muddled by this overwhelming urge to indulge her curiosity in another human being. Curiosity, she now thought, complicated things, left her with a headache.

'I suppose they would,' Grant drawled, staring at her, 'but you're not.'

Roberta laughed shortly. 'I'd be impressed if you managed to find me a way out of here.'

'Well, I'm afraid I don't run to miracles,' he said tersely. 'Now, would you mind passing me my case?'

She handed it to him and he snapped it open, extracting a disk and several sheets of paper. Then he walked across to the desk in the far corner of the room and switched on the computer terminal.

'And instead of twiddling your thumbs and praying for a break in the snow,' he said, without raising his head, 'why don't you do something about lunch? There's a lot in the kitchen. And you'd better get out of those clothes. They're damp. If you stay in them much longer, you'll probably end up with pneumonia and find that you can't move out of here when the snow finally does let up.'

This was a new variation on a problem. She stared at him aghast.

'But I haven't brought any clothes with me,' she said.

He barely glanced at her. She might just as well have been a piece of furniture, she thought, wondering whether that made her feel relieved or piqued.

'There are some of my things in the dresser,' he muttered, his face wearing an expression of intense concentration as he stared at whatever the screen had thrown up for him.

Roberta sighed and walked towards the dresser, rummaging about in the bottom drawer until she pulled out a long-sleeved T-shirt with a baseball motto on the front.

It would do. It had obviously done for someone else before her and, from the size of it, it hadn't been Grant. She vanished into the bedroom, pulling off her damp clothes and slipping on the T-shirt, which fitted her perfectly apart from the length. Whoever had worn this had been taller than her.

She looked at herself in the free-standing mirror on the wooden dressing-table, one of the few concessions to vanity in the house, and tried to ignore the brightness in her eyes and the hectic colour in her cheeks.

Grant didn't look up as she re-entered the room. It was only as she walked past him on the way to the kitchen that he glanced at her, his eyes narrowing as he took in her slender body under the baggy cotton.

'Where did you get that?' he grated. 'Where the hell did you get that?'

'In the dresser,' Roberta replied coolly, even though the dangerous glitter in his eyes was making her feel increasingly apprehensive. She remembered that thunderous rage which had filled him when he had first seen her. She didn't need a repetition of that out here in the middle of nowhere.

She stepped backwards unconsciously and said, in a quick, defensive voice, 'I only looked where you told me to. It was the only thing I could find that would fit me. I can hardly be expected to walk around in a pair of your trousers, can I?'

'Get it off!' he ordered, standing over her and supporting the weight of his body on the table, his features rigid with fury.

'Why?'

'Because I'm telling you to.'

She took another few steps backwards. Right now he looked as though he could throttle her, in which case she had no intention of deliberately standing in his line of fire.

'Look,' she said, attempting to defuse the situation, 'aren't you over-reacting just a little? It's just a T-shirt, for heaven's sake!' She gave him a weak smile, quailing visibly as he took a step towards her.

'If you don't take that damned thing off, then I'll do it for you,' he muttered, and he meant it. She could see the intent as clearly in his eyes as if it had been scrawled in bright red lettering across his forehead.

Her feet froze to the ground as his hand clasped her arm, moving to the neckline of the T-shirt. Galvanised into action, she struggled against him, her efforts bringing them both to the floor in an undignified heap.

Then her bewilderment and anger was replaced by something altogether different. An intense longing that ripped through her body as his fingers found the tiny buttons on the front of the T-shirt and began undoing them.

She was breathing quickly, her face flushed, and he must have noticed the intangible change in her because, just as quickly, his fury gave way to a stifled moan and the fingers that had been tugging at the buttons curved to cup the nape of her neck.

She knew that he was going to kiss her even before his lips found hers, and she knew as well that she was powerless to fight it.

That deep-seated attraction which she had felt for him ever since they had first met had clearly been simmering away inside her, waiting to erupt, and his mouth, moving feverishly over hers, was the catalyst that unlocked it.

She gave a tiny groan and closed her eyes, succumbing to his plundering tongue. Her hands coiled upwards to caress his head and she felt as though she had been waiting for this moment for all her life. Nothing had prepared her for this. Not Brian, not anyone. This torrent of desperate yearning was quite new to her.

It seemed to fill her body, making her thoughts, her power to reason, hazy and ineffective.

And when she felt his hand slide along the smoothness of her thighs, she lost the ability to think at all.

CHAPTER SIX

THERE were a thousand reasons why she should stop him before the situation reached the point of no return, but for the life of her she couldn't recall any of them. It was as if all her normal processes of reasoning had been suddenly suspended in mid-air. She knew that they would all come flooding back to her, probably sooner rather than later, but right now they were tantalisingly out of reach.

He slid his hand into her hair, and murmured huskily, 'The floor isn't exactly the ideal place to make love, is it?'

A wave of recklessness washed over her. 'It seems fine to me.'

'The bedroom is only yards away. But now that you're in my arms I don't want to let you go even for that short distance.'

'I could always lift you there,' Roberta teased, and he chuckled under his breath.

'I'm six feet two and not exactly lightly built.'

'I know,' she whispered with shameless abandon, running her fingers down his spine and pulling his shirt out of the waistband of his trousers. He had not changed his clothes, and they were slightly damp, but the moistness of his skin only aroused her further.

She pulled his head towards her and kissed him with feverish passion, while her fingers fumbled with the buttons of his shirt until they were all undone and he shrugged it off.

GET 4 BOOKS
A CUDDLY TEDDY
AND A MYSTERY GIFT

Return this card, and we'll send you 4 Mills & Boon Romances, absolutely FREE! We'll even pay the postage and packing for you!

We're making you this offer to introduce you to the benefits of Mills & Boon Reader Service: free home delivery of brand-new Romance novels, at least a month before they're available in the shops, FREE gifts and a monthly Newsletter packed with offers and information.

Accepting these 4 free books places you under no obligation to buy, you may cancel at any time, even just after receiving your free shipment.

Yes, please send me 4 free Mills & Boon Romances, a Cuddly Teddy and a Mystery Gift as explained above. Please also reserve a Reader Service Subscription for me. If I decide to subscribe, I shall receive six superb new titles every month for just £10.20 postage & packing free. If I decide not to subscribe I shall write to you within 10 days. The free books and gifts will be mine to keep in any case. I understand that I am under no obligation whatsoever. I may cancel or suspend my subscription at any time simply by writing to you.

Ms/Mrs/Miss/Mr _____ 4A3R

Address _____

_____

_____ Postcode_____

Signature_____
I am over 18 years of age.

Get 4 Books
a Cuddly Teddy and
Mystery Gift FREE!

SEE BACK OF CARD FOR DETAILS

Mills & Boon Reader Service,
FREEPOST
P.O. Box 236
Croydon
CR9 9EL

Offer expires 31st August 1993. One per household. The right is reserved to refuse an application and change the terms of this offer. Offer applies to U.K. and Eire only. Readers overseas please send for details. Southern Africa write to: Book Services International Ltd., P.O. Box 41654 Craighall, Transvaal 2024. You may be mailed with offers from other reputable companies as a result of this application. You may be mailed with offers from other reputable companies as a result of this application. If you would prefer not to share these opportunities, please tick this box. □

MPS
MAILING
PREFERENCE
SERVICE

No
stamp
needed

How had she ever imagined that she had tasted the exquisite fruit of desire? What little experience she had had paled into insignificance next to what she was feeling now.

He tilted her head backwards and trailed his mouth along her neck, his hand slipping underneath the T-shirt to caress the fullness of her breasts.

Roberta shuddered as his fingers found the hardened tip of her nipple.

'I think the bed will have to wait after all,' he said roughly. Expertly, he freed her shoulders from the T-shirt, pulling it down until she was naked, then he drew back, his eyes roving with restless thoroughness over her body.

Roberta smiled. She had always been slightly inhibited about her body. She felt none of those inhibitions now as she lay back provocatively, enjoying the fire of his scrutiny.

He traced a line along her thigh, pausing to stroke the flat contours of her stomach, and by the time his finger reached her breast she was gasping for breath.

'I've tried to imagine what lay under that control of yours,' he murmured, his breathing as uneven as her own. 'I've never met any woman who didn't invite with her body, but not you. I couldn't begin to think what it would be like to make love with you.'

He caressed her breasts with his mouth until she felt the warm wetness of his tongue flicking over her nipple. The sensation was overwhelming, beyond description. Had she really lived before this? It seemed not.

He shrugged off his trousers, still teasing her breasts with his mouth and, as she felt the hardness of his body alongside hers, Roberta felt as though, in some strange way, she had come home. Their bodies felt so right together.

She ran her hands along his back, curling her fingers in his hair as he travelled lower to explore her entire body with sensuous passion.

He was a considerate lover, unhurriedly rousing her to a pitch of excitement which she had never before experienced, even though his hunger was every bit as consuming as her own.

He pressed his face against her stomach and she whimpered, her feet moving restlessly against his thighs.

Every caress was so exquisite that it almost hurt and, as he moved upwards to claim her mouth with a savage kiss, Roberta moaned into his ear, 'Please, I can't hold out much longer. I want you so much.'

She had no idea what furious instinct was driving her on, but she did know that she couldn't have stopped now even if she had wanted to.

Nor could he. She felt the weight of his body on hers, and her fingers pressed into his back, urging him on until his fierce, rhythmic movements took her over the edge of ecstasy. Ripples of pleasure swept through her, finally ebbing, and she looked at him from under her lashes.

His green eyes languorously returned her stare and he smiled, a crooked little smile that made her senses swim all over again.

'I won't throw you all those clichéd questions about whether the earth moved for you,' he murmured huskily, 'but I'll tell you that it damned well did for me.'

'Did it?' She raised her wide grey eyes to his and he laughed softly under his breath.

'You're a witch,' he told her, 'a siren.'

'I've never been called that before. Is it meant as a compliment?'

'Figure it out for yourself.'

Figure it out? She wasn't up to figuring anything out at the moment. Her brain had not yet got into gear.

She smiled at him drowsily and stroked his black hair, wanting time to stand still so that her brain never had to get into gear. She had been swept off to another planet with his lovemaking and, if she had her way, she would stay right there for the rest of her life.

Outside the snow had abated, but it was dusky inside the cabin, despite the fact that it was only the middle of the afternoon. The fire which he had earlier lit had flooded the place with warmth, though. She had no desire to get back into her clothes.

'You certainly made your point,' she said, and he stared at her, bemused.

'Point? What point?'

'You wanted me out of that T-shirt, and you had your way after all.' The merest flicker of a shadow crossed his features, and she asked lazily, 'Why did you react so violently when you saw me wearing it?'

If she had been thinking straight, she would have foreseen the answer long before the question had even been asked, but her mind was muddled, so when he did reply it came as a shock.

'It reminded me of Vivian.'

One little sentence that hovered on the edge of her brain and then shot in, blinding her with its impact.

'It reminded you of your ex-wife,' she repeated in a hollow voice.

'It belonged to her. I have no idea how it remained at the bottom of that dresser. I guess I never cleared it out and, since I only use the stuff in there very irregularly, I just never came across it.'

That warm afterglow that she had been feeling only moments before evaporated like early-morning mist. Now, there was a sour taste in her mouth that made her want to retch.

'Was that why you made love to me?' she asked acidly. 'Because I reminded you of your wife?'

Grant faced her, his body stiffening at her tone of voice.

'I wasn't making love to a memory, if that's what you're implying,' he said tightly.

'Weren't you? Well, it very much sounds that way to me.'

'You asked me a question and I answered it. Would you rather I had lied?'

Roberta wriggled out of his embrace, pulling on her underwear with jerky movements. She looked at the wretched T-shirt with loathing, as if it had some unpleasant life of its own, and walked across to where she had laid out her clothes to dry, hastily slipping on her own shirt and her pair of jeans, which were no longer damp.

She knew that Grant had twisted around, was watching her every movement. He stood up and moved across to her, not bothering to get dressed, and she kept her eyes rigorously averted.

'Well, answer me!' he demanded, yanking a towel out of the dresser and wrapping it around his waist. 'Would you have rather I had lied?'

The anger brewing inside her was partly directed at him, but mostly it was directed at herself, because she should never have allowed their lovemaking to happen. She could have stopped it. He would not have forced her. But, like a fool, she had stuck her head in the sand

and pretended that no problems existed, because she could not see them, or rather had not wanted to see them.

She had courted disaster with a reckless disregard for common sense, and she was paying the price for her mistake.

She thought of Brian, of her foolishness, which had blinded her to reason, and then she thought of Grant. And the similiarity between the two situations made her want to throw up.

She looked at him scathingly. 'By all means, tell the truth,' she bit out. 'Honesty is always the best policy, isn't it?'

He approached her and she stood her ground. Where could she run? Running, anyway, would not have solved anything. She could run a million miles, and the pain she was feeling now would still be as acute.

'Obviously not in this instance,' he grated. 'Does it make a difference, anyway? We made love, that's something that you can't deny, and——'

'Deny it?' she yelled. 'Who's trying to deny anything?' She took a few deep breaths to steady herself, and at the end of it she still felt like throwing things. 'I must have been mad,' she whispered.

'What's so mad about doing something that you want?' he threw at her. 'Do you intend to take refuge behind that mask of yours for the rest of your life, just because you happen to have had one bad experience with a man?'

'And stop acting as though you know what motivates me,' she said fiercely.

'What did he do to you?' he pursued relentlessly.

Roberta stared at him silently, then she turned away with a weary gesture.

'Look,' she said, controlling the tremor in her voice, 'I'm not looking for involvement——'

'Nor am I.' He stepped towards her and she looked at him coldly.

She knew what was going on in his mind. As far as he was concerned, neither of them were looking for involvement, so where did the problem lie? He had told her that she only saw things in black and white, but right now that was exactly how he was seeing things. He fancied her, and she had been stupid enough to show him that the attraction was mutual, so why not make love? Sex for him was quite distinct from emotional commitment. It was an act of pleasure, a meeting of two bodies. Commitment, she thought bitterly, was something he reserved for his dead wife.

His experienced, seductive touch had sent her spinning off to another planet, and the inevitable bump back to reality hurt. She thought of Brian. What was the point of learning lessons if you then rushed head-first into the same mistake?

Grant was not a con man; he lacked Brian's calculating deviousness. No doubt he really believed that he played fair by telling his Vanessas that he was out of bounds. But underneath it all, weren't they both alike?

She felt devalued and miserable.

'There's no point discussing what happened,' she said, struggling to fight down that sick feeling inside her. 'It was all a big mistake. Now, do you mind just dropping the subject?'

'Yes, I mind!' he grated, raking his fingers impatiently through his hair. 'We made love and you stand there, prepared to act as though nothing had happened.'

'Has it slipped your mind that you have a girlfriend?' Roberta threw at him, and he looked at her blankly, as though he couldn't quite figure out how that fitted into anything at all.

'There's no commitment there.'

'How convenient,' she said coolly. 'Do you think that Vanessa would see it from that point of view?'

'Do you think,' he returned, 'that you could stop acting like an enraged virgin who's just been raped?'

There was a long silence, then Roberta walked off towards the kitchen to prepare something to eat. She was still trembling, still disgusted with herself for having given in to a physical urge with a man who made no effort to hide the fact that sex, for him, was a temporary pleasure. A matter of course.

But she didn't really blame him. She blamed herself. She should have known better. The recrimination rang through her head until she just wanted to find somewhere dark and private where she could cry her eyes out.

But there was no such escape and she would never cry in front of him. Never.

She wondered where they would have gone from here had she not reacted the way that she did. Would he have happily conducted a love-affair with her until she was ready to leave, waved goodbye at the airport, then taken up the reins of his life with the next woman in the queue? The thought made her sick.

She stared outside. At least there was little chance of her being pregnant. Not at this time of the month. Wouldn't that, she thought, have been the final, crushing defeat?

The furious onslaught of snow had died down to a half-hearted flurry. The car, though, was still shrouded in white, but with any luck she would be out of this place by tomorrow. Beyond that she did not care to think.

Lunch, as well as being extremely late, was a silent affair, the conversation stilted, with Roberta unable to meet his eyes.

The computer terminal, which Roberta had originally thought highly incongruous in the setting of a distant cabin, proved a blessing in disguise. It spared her the discomfort of having to talk to him in a neutral tone of voice for the remainder of the day. He worked on it, frowning in concentration, and she read an outdated Western paperback which she found lying about.

Or rather, she made a valiant effort to read, but shutting her mind to the disturbing thoughts flitting about inside was impossible. Had she agonised this much after her disastrous affair with Brian? She couldn't recall. When she tried to summon up an image of him, she failed. All she could see was Grant's black hair, his vivid eyes, and that cynical twist to his mouth, which could change with alarming suddenness into a smile of unbearable charm.

Dinner was an equally stony affair. She asked him how his work was coming along, and he replied that it was all wrapped up, not that it made much difference since it was unlikely that the meeting would be held the following day anyway.

I could have been spared all this, Roberta thought bitterly. Wasn't fate capricious?

'Are you still tired?' she asked, scouring her mind for something to say.

Grant sat back and looked at her. 'Not any longer. Maybe I've just gone past the point of physical exhaustion, or maybe there's another reason.'

That was enough to make her stand up and busy herself clearing away the dishes, refusing his offer of assistance. She didn't want to have to look at those powerful hands and to be reminded of how they had made her feel.

'I'm off to bed now,' she said, when the kitchen was tidy and the only other option facing her was the outdated Western.

He nodded, his back to her, and she scurried off to the bedroom with a sigh of relief. She was beginning to fall into a light sleep when the door opened, and her body tensed immediately.

She sensed rather than saw him start removing his clothes, and she sat up abruptly.

'And I thought you were asleep,' he said drily, standing in front of her with just his trousers on.

'What are you doing?'

'What does it look like I'm doing? I'm about to get into bed.'

'Not this bed, you're not.'

'And where else do you suggest I sleep?' he asked coldly. 'In case you haven't realised, this is the only bedroom, and that's the only bed.'

He unzipped his trousers and she looked away. She felt the bed depress under his weight as he sank on to it, and she stared at him, horrified.

'I don't care!' she shot out. Under the duvet, she knew that he was completely naked, and the thought frightened her to death. 'Why can't you sleep in the living-room?'

In an effortless movement his hand reached out to grasp her wrist, his eyes glittering in the darkness.

'One bedroom,' he grated, 'one bed, one duvet. If you don't like it, then you're free to go somewhere else, though I wouldn't recommend it. When that fire dies, this place will become freezing cold, and I have no intention of dealing with hypothermia. Now, do you lie back down or do I have to pin you down forcibly?'

Roberta glared at him with helpless fury, but she lay down nevertheless.

Underneath the crisp cotton man's shirt which she had taken out of the dressing-table, she could feel her heart beating painfully. How was she supposed to fall asleep, knowing that he was in the same bed as her? Naked?

'Just make sure that you...' She searched around for the right words, and he found them for her.

'Keep my hands to myself?'

She didn't reply, and he continued with a trace of ice in his voice, 'Rest assured I won't touch you. You can huddle in your pristine little corner of the bed, nursing your grievances, in peace.'

His words stung, brought a flush of colour to her face.

'Good,' she muttered.

'I don't go around forcing myself on unwilling women. I don't have the need.'

'I'm sure you don't!' Roberta snapped.

He ignored her outburst. 'And I certainly have no time for women who make love and then try and make out that, Oh, dear, it's all been a horrible misadventure, what on earth came over me? I'm really not that type of girl.'

He was mocking her, his voice a cynical mimicry of prim horror, and Roberta flinched. Was that how he saw her? Probably. She knew that she had given him every reason, with her burning response to him, that she was quite willing to play his sophisticated games of love, no strings attached.

'That's not fair,' Roberta said in a small voice.

He had turned on his side to face her, and she stared upwards at the ceiling, feeling his breath on her face, uncomfortably aware that if she did look at him, that overpowering, pointless attraction that she felt for him might begin to work again.

'Isn't it? And how do I know that you're not playing hard to get for a reason?'

'What?'

'Perhaps you think that a challenge is more enticing to a man than an easy catch.'

Roberta looked at him, speechless.

'That's a nasty thing to say,' she finally whispered. 'It's also untrue.'

'Prove it,' he murmured huskily. He reached out to stroke the curtain of hair away from her face, and she flinched back.

'I told you, I made a mistake. I didn't mean to let things get so far.'

'And where did you want to stop, exactly?' he asked in a hard voice, removing his hand. 'Before I took your clothes off, or maybe just slightly afterwards? Don't you know that it's dangerous to give a man a taste of honey and then whip it away? Do you think that if you hold out for long enough, I might promise you something?'

'I don't want to hear any more of this.' She covered her ears with her hands and squeezed her eyes shut tightly.

With a swift movement, he pulled her hand away, and when he spoke his voice was laden with intent. 'Nobody plays games with me, lady. You might have your reasons for retreat, but you've whetted my appetite. Just remember that. This won't be the last time that we share a bed, and the next time I might not be quite so restrained.'

Was that a threat? Roberta wanted to ask because, if it was, she wasn't going to bend under it. He might go through life pulling all the strings, but she had no intention of becoming another of his disposable women.

She pointedly turned over, so that she was staring at the wall, waiting for him to prolong his attack, but nothing came, and after a while she was aware from his deep, regular breathing that he had fallen asleep.

A thin grey light was filtering through the curtains when she woke up the following morning. It took her a second of blissful unawareness before she remembered that she had not slept alone in the bed the night before, then she twisted around quickly, expelling a long sigh of relief at the empty spot next to her.

Where was he now? She didn't dwell on the matter for too long, just in case he surprised her in the bedroom. There was no lock on the door, and the last thing she needed in her fragile state of mind was to have to face him in a state of undress.

She found the cabin empty and, pouring herself a cup of black coffee, she strolled across to the window and stared outside. Definite improvement in the conditions there. No fresh snow had fallen, and he had scraped the car completely. What time had he got up? she wondered. It was now only just after eight o'clock.

It made her uncomfortable to think of him getting up, looking at her as she lay sleeping, thinking God only knew what, and she turned away abruptly.

It was another hour before he reappeared, and as soon as she saw the door open Roberta felt her body tense. He was wearing the same pair of trousers which he had travelled up in, but the olive-green chunky sweater and the well-worn waterproof coat had obviously come from the cabin. They suited him.

Roberta eyed him as he crossed the lounge.

'I'm sorry I wasn't up earlier to help you,' she said awkwardly, relieved that there was nothing hostile in his face when he looked back at her. Maybe, she thought, he had considered what she had said and realised that what had happened the day before had been an unfortunate slip up.

'No problem.' He shrugged, moving to pour himself a cup of coffee. 'There was nothing I couldn't handle on my own.'

He had not shaved and the stubble darkening his chin gave him a rakish appearance. Was it really any wonder, looking like that, that he was so confident when it came to the opposite sex?

She caught his eye, and it was on the tip of her tongue to make a teasing quip about his lack of modesty, but she refrained, only realising that he had followed her train of thought exactly when he raised one eyebrow with dry amusement.

'Do you think we'll be able to leave this morning?' she asked hurriedly. She could keep her composure if there were no personal undercurrents running between them. That complicated things, made her uneasy and self-conscious, and far too aware of his lethal brand of sexuality for her own good. And when that happened it was as if some key in her had been turned, winding her up and making her act out of character.

He gave the matter a few minutes' thought. 'There's been no snow overnight,' he said slowly, 'and the road's bad, but not totally impassable. Of course, it'll take us some time to get to the main road, but once we're there we shouldn't have a problem. The main road will be clear enough for traffic.'

'And your meeting?'

'Has been rearranged.'

'Has it?'

'I called the people concerned to tell them that it was off.'

Roberta smiled, relaxing at this undemanding strain of small talk. 'I bet they must have loved you waking them up at some ungodly hour in the morning,' she said.

'They're accustomed to it. They don't receive massive salaries for nine-to-five days. Mr Ishikomo was decidedly relieved not to have to face a journey in this weather. I don't think he likes our Canadian snow very much.'

He walked towards the kitchen to wash up his mug and Roberta followed him with her eyes, sensible enough to realise that it was too easy to be lulled into a false sense of security when he was like this. She was in full command of herself now, but one look from him, one unnecessary touch, had the ability of making her foundations very shaky.

He began packing a bag with tinned food, and she asked ingenuously, 'What's that for?'

'Emergency provisions,' he threw over his shoulder. 'It pays to be cautious in this weather. Have you got any likes or dislikes when it comes to cans?'

She approached him and stood a few feet away, surveying the stock which he obligingly held up one by one for her inspection. Corned beef, tuna, salmon, crackers, beans of various description.

'Is all that really necessary?' she asked doubtfully. 'There's enough food there to feed the starving millions.'

He laughed at that, a deep-throated laugh that made her mouth go dry.

When he had finished, he hand-picked two bottles of wine and carefully placed them on top. 'If you're stuck in snow,' he drawled, 'you might as well freeze to death in a good mood.'

She grinned reluctantly, not wanting to respond to him, not wanting to like him, but finding it difficult to be churlish.

He had started the engine of the car, and when they finally slipped into the seats it was beautifully warm. He was driving. She had probably, he said, seen enough of their wintry driving conditions to last a lifetime.

Just clearing the small road out was arduous. They moved at a snail's pace, creeping along while the dark skies threatened more snow. It was only when they at last made it to the main road that she felt him relax next to her, and they built up a bit more speed.

Roberta lay back against the seat and closed her eyes, and gradually settled into a light doze. When she next opened her eyes, it was to discover that the car had stopped, and Grant was staring at her with an odd expression in his eyes. He turned away abruptly and she asked, dazed, 'Have we arrived back already?'

'That's a bit optimistic,' he said drily. 'I thought that since we didn't eat anything for breakfast we might as well stop off here for a bite.'

Roberta rubbed her eyes and yawned, still languorous with sleep. 'Must we?' She yawned again. 'Anyway, I'm surprised you can't rustle something up one-handed with all those cans you packed. Scrambled eggs, mushrooms and pancakes out of two tins of salmon and a pack of biscuits.' She stretched, blushing in confusion when he said lazily,

'You ought to sleep more often in a car. You wake up in a decidedly humorous frame of mind.'

The lazy teasing in his voice got rid of her last vestiges of drowsiness and she looked around her, her eyes finally resting on the small diner he had stopped in front of.

When he came around to open her door for her she peered at him suspiciously, very tempted to ask, why are you being so nice? Had he completely forgotten the accusations and bitterness that had seethed between them the night before?

She didn't trust this sudden change from aggressive anger to easy charm. It unsettled her, made her think that she ought to be on the look-out for sudden moves. He was, she thought, the equivalent of a well-fed tiger: temporarily content, but only a fool would ignore its latent danger.

She edged past him quickly, only falling into step as they approached the small diner which turned out to be cheerful and quite full, mostly with men who all seemed to be on a first-name basis with the waitresses.

They sat at a small table and Roberta ravenously consumed a plateful of glorious, sizzling Canadian streaky bacon, a fried egg and four slices of toast.

'Maybe I was just a little hungry after all,' she said defensively, catching the amused expression on his face.

'I've never met a woman who ate as much as you do,' he said, leaning back in the chair and folding his arms. 'Where do you put it all? Or perhaps I know.'

Roberta looked at him sharply, but his face was bland. So this was what he was up to, was it? A cat and mouse game with him as the predatory cat, and herself in the role of frightened mouse.

He hadn't relegated the events of the previous day to some dusty, cold storage unit at the back of his mind, as she had naïvely supposed.

After all, hadn't he told her fiercely that she had whetted his appetite? He was biding his time, circling her like a waiting bird of prey, rising to what he saw as the challenge of getting her into bed, for his own personal amusement.

Well, it wasn't going to work.

She wiped her mouth on her serviette and stood up. 'I think we ought to be setting off. I'd like to get back as quickly as possible so that I can make sure that Emily's all right.'

She stuck her hands into her jacket pockets, clenching them into a tight ball. She had got his measure now. He intended to deploy the full brunt of that formidable charm on her, she was sure of it, but, as he got closer, so she would back away.

He signalled to the waitress for the bill, and she pointedly ignored the glint in his green eyes as they scanned her body.

She would be polite with him till the cows came home, she thought, throwing him a very controlled smile and then quickly shifting her eyes away from his. He seemed to have the unnerving ability to read her thoughts, and she wasn't going to let him.

Oh, no, as far as she was concerned, this was all-out war, and she would have much more to lose than him if she didn't win it.

Why, she thought irritably, couldn't he have fitted into the stereotype of the paunchy, middle-aged tycoon that she had expected? The very least people could do was live down to your expectations.

They resumed the journey, with the soft music on the radio providing a soothing backdrop to her thoughts.

She was inordinately relieved when the car finally pulled up outside the house. She slung open her door and hurried up to the front door, impatiently waiting for him to open it, eager to get out of the claustrophobic confines of his company.

As he pushed open the door she stepped inside, the expression on her face changing into one of horror as she stared at the mess around her. Empty bottles in the hall, an ashtray crammed with dead cigarette butts, the smell of smoke still lingering in the air, tainting it with its peculiar, acrid smell.

'What the hell . . . ?' Grant said from behind her. He stepped in, and then repeated, in a dangerously soft voice, 'What the hell has been going on here?'

CHAPTER SEVEN

ROBERTA didn't look at him. She didn't want to see that thunderous rage on his face. She had a pretty shrewd idea of what had taken place in the house, and she suspected that he had as well.

She opened her mouth to begin a conciliatory little speech, something along the lines of being patient and understanding, but she didn't get as far as the first syllable. He muttered, 'Where's my daughter?' and she watched worriedly as he strode past her, taking the stairs two by two, his hand impatiently skimming the banister.

She remained standing where she was. She could already hear the inevitable confrontation happening above her, the sound of Emily's raised voice, slamming of doors, but she had no part in any of it. It was a family affair and, helpless though she felt, all she could do was stay put and hope that nothing came crashing through the floorboards overhead.

It wasn't terribly difficult to recall the rage of which he was capable and, whoever was to blame for the dead cigarette butts and the evidence of drinking, she still felt sorry for Emily. She had a suspicion that his daughter would be tried and convicted without much of a hearing in between.

It wasn't, she knew, that Grant didn't love his daughter. He did. It was simply that he could not channel that love into the right methods of expression.

It was hard enough trying to communicate with a teenager, but in this instance the lines of communication were so fragile that they frequently faced each other like warring adversaries, neither capable of the sort of reasonable discussion that solved most problems.

The crashing and slamming had subsided into an ominous silence and Roberta held her breath, waiting. She didn't have long to wait. Grant reappeared at the top of the staircase, his hand clutching a young boy who looked scared to death. Behind them, there was a girl of about the same age, also visibly quailing. Of Emily there was no sign.

Grant roughly half dragged, half pulled him down the stairs, while the boy fumbled with his coat, attempting to put it on, which was an impossible manoeuvre.

'What's going on?' Roberta asked, running up to them, her eyes anxious. 'Is this really necessary?' she asked Grant quietly, hanging on to her calm in the face of all this mayhem.

His face twisted into a snarl. 'Keep out of it!'

So much for the charm, she thought. He was as mad as hell, and making no attempt to conceal it.

'As for you,' he addressed the unfortunate youth, who was now eyeing the front door with desperate zeal, 'I don't want to see you show your face here again. Is that quite clear?'

The boy nodded rapidly, and the girl, who had been hovering behind, sprinted towards the door, opening it and letting herself out quickly. Poor girl, Roberta thought, she doesn't know what's hit her. Grant in a foul temper was much more than merely alarming. He was formidable.

He slammed the front door behind them, and then turned to face her.

'And you try to tell me that my daughter is capable of reasonable behaviour?' He was barely articulate in his anger. 'One night!' he spluttered. 'One night, and this is what happens.' He shot her an expression that made her feel that somehow she was responsible for Emily's conduct.

'Have you talked to her about it?' Roberta asked calmly. 'What did she have to say by way of explanation?'

'And don't you stand there and question me!' he roared. 'You can see for yourself what kind of a state the house is in! I'm going to pack her off to the strictest boarding-school I can find in the country! If she thinks she can waltz through life doing what the hell she wants, with no thought for other people, then she's got another think coming!' He glared at her, speechless.

'You still haven't told me what she said,' Roberta pointed out reasonably. She turned away and began clearing the ashtrays from the tables, carrying them into the kitchen, while he followed her, his anger radiating in waves from him like a forcefield.

'And I suppose you think that I haven't handled this properly!' he thundered from behind her. 'You don't have to say anything! It's written all over that cool little face of yours!'

Roberta emptied the cigarette ash into the bin, and began stacking the used glasses which were lying all over the kitchen counters into the sink.

He was deliberately needling her, she realised, trying to provoke a reaction out of her so that he could get his teeth into something and have an excuse for really letting fly. She had no intention of giving him any such excuse. Emotionally, and physically, she might be vulnerable to him, but right now she was very much in control and that was how she intended to stay.

'You could help by bringing those bottles into the kitchen and sticking them into the bin,' she informed him without looking around.

He ignored her, not moving from where he was standing by the kitchen counter.

'Look,' she said with a sigh, 'getting angry isn't going to solve anything, is it?'

'Oh?' he jeered. 'Let's just use your method of compassionate understanding, shall we? Let's just be collected and then try leaving Emily again for another night on her own and see what happens, shall we?'

Roberta met his stare. 'That's an idea,' she mused, giving it consideration. 'We might find ourselves pleasantly surprised.'

He was calmer now. That frightening anger had left him, but she knew that his whiplash in a calm frame of mind could be equally potent.

'I tried with that girl,' he muttered under his breath. 'It's not easy bringing up a daughter on your own.'

'You're not on your own,' Roberta pointed out. 'Your mother lives with you.'

'You know exactly what I mean, so don't try and pretend that you don't. Not that you would understand anyway—you have no children of your own. It's always easy to preach about right and wrong when you're not personally involved.'

He watched her while she continued to tidy the kitchen. Teenagers, she thought, really were capable of a great deal of mess. They seemed to operate on the theory of why use one glass when four will do, and why bother to wash up when there's more clean crockery where the last lot came from?

Still, it was disturbing to speculate on what had happened. She would give Emily time to calm down from her father's onslaught, and then she would try and wade her way through the inevitable sullen defensiveness until she arrived at some sort of explanation.

Maybe he was right, maybe it was easier to be logical when you weren't personally involved, but that didn't mean that you didn't care, and it didn't mean that the advice you offered was worthless.

Right now, though, that would have been the last thing that he would have been inclined to hear.

She remained silent, until he snapped, 'Well, are you just going to stand there washing dishes, or are you going to say something? You're partly responsible for Emily's behaviour while you're under this roof, don't forget.'

'That line of argument doesn't wash with me,' Roberta said crossly. 'I've had no hand in shaping her moral values. My role here is primarily supervisory.'

'Oh, very convenient, your taking that stance all of a sudden, isn't it?' He crossed over to where she was standing and leaned indolently against the counter, watching her with a cynical expression. 'You weren't backward about lecturing to me about what I was doing wrong with Emily when you first arrived, though, were you? Oh, no. For someone whose role here is solely supervisory, you made your opinions quite clear from the word go, didn't you?'

'You're her father,' Roberta informed him bluntly. 'You're responsible for how she turns out. She takes her cue from you.'

'There you go again.' He glared at her. 'Miss Know-it-all of the Year.'

'I'm merely stating the obvious.'

'It's no wonder that man left you high and dry,' he muttered by way of response. 'You probably bossed the life out of him with your "I know what's best" attitude.'

Roberta turned off the tap and slowly faced him. 'That's below the belt,' she said, controlling her anger with difficulty.

He had the grace to flush, his eyes shifting away from hers.

'Yes,' he admitted, sticking his hands into his pockets. 'It was. I apologise. But what do you expect when you hoard your secrets like a little squirrel hoarding its stash of nuts?'

Roberta looked at him, wondering how she could ever have found his charm and humour so irresistible. Right now, she felt like thumping him with the nearest available object. Preferably one that was very hard and would have a very lasting effect.

How had the conversation come round to this subject, anyway? One minute he had been shouting his head off about Emily, the next he had managed to drag her personal life into it, as though it had some part in his fury.

'I didn't realise,' she said, meeting his eyes and holding them with her own, 'that I was being paid to give you the story of my life.'

He looked at her oddly and looked away.

'Well,' he muttered, 'well, you see if you can talk to her. You're a woman, you try.' He walked off towards the door, throwing over his shoulder before he left, 'You know so damned much, you have a go.'

He slammed the kitchen door behind him, and Roberta was left feeling as though she didn't quite know what the hell had taken place between them just then.

She shrugged her shoulders and told herself that it really didn't matter. In a lot of ways, he was a mystery, one that she would not unravel, but in one very important aspect he was just a man, a man who operated on a love them and leave them level, and that was something that she should make sure never to forget.

She finished clearing away the debris, and then made her way upstairs, wondering what sort of state she would find Emily in.

Quite self-possessed and, as she had expected, on the defensive.

'It's you,' she said, throwing herself on the bed and subjecting Roberta to a baleful glare, 'and I suppose you've come up here to have a go?'

'What makes you think that?'

'Well, it seems to be my day, doesn't it? Dad flying in here like a tornado, whipping out my friends as though they were armed robbers.' She gave a dour laugh. 'I'm surprised he didn't put them under house arrest and get the police involved. It wouldn't have surprised me.' She looked at Roberta sullenly and her bottom lip quivered for a second.

'You have to try and understand it from his point of view,' Roberta began, tentatively trying to feel out a good middle ground.

'Why? Why should I? He didn't see it from my point of view. In fact, he just stormed in here and yelled as though I were a five-year-old kid wrecking the furniture with her box of paints. That's always been his style, though. He lays down the law and people follow it.'

Two bright spots of anger had appeared on her cheeks just from the experience of reliving her father's reaction.

'There was an awful lot of mess,' Roberta said quietly. 'Glasses everywhere. Ashtrays filled with cigarette butts. I didn't know you smoked.'

'And that's another thing,' Emily burst out. She clearly had a lot to say on what had happened and, now that she was being given a hearing, couldn't wait to create her own minor explosion. Roberta suspected that she had been so cowed by her father that she had taken refuge in sullen silence, which of course would have just stoked his fury further. 'He came on strong, yelling and shouting about smoking under his roof, that it was disgusting, that if that was what I learned from boarding-school then he would damn well make sure that the next one was as disciplinarian as a prison. He didn't stop to ask whether I was the one smoking or not.'

'And were you?' Roberta asked interestedly.

'Of course not! I wouldn't touch the stuff. Ugh!'

'So what exactly happened?'

Emily gave the matter some thought, as if debating whether Roberta was on her side or on the side of the enemy. 'When Dad phoned,' she finally said, 'and told me that you two were stuck in his cabin, I decided to have a couple of friends over. Just to watch a video or something. Except, things got out of hand. One of my girlfriends brought her brother, who brought some of his friends, who brought some bottles of wine and some cans of beer and before I knew it the place was being turned upside-down. I really did try to get them out...' Her voice trailed off and Roberta nodded.

'I believe you.'

'You're just saying that!'

'I'm not. Honestly. I know that you're a horrible little thing, but I would never have believed you to have any part in an evening of smoking and drinking.'

'Horrible little thing?' Emily's face relaxed into the shadow of a grin. 'That's rude!'

'Oh, but I can afford to be rude,' Roberta said with a smile. 'I'm only the au pair.'

'Anyway, those two friends that Dad dragged out of the house were as innocent as I was. They probably don't know what hit them. They'll never speak to me again.'

'Course they will. You just said, they're your friends.'

Emily looked at her seriously. 'I'm glad you're here,' she said with touching honesty. 'At least I have someone between me and Dad.'

Roberta laughed. 'Is that part of my job description? Buffer? I'll have to give the matter some careful thought. You should try and explain things to your father, you know.'

'Never!'

'Why not?'

'Because,' Emily said patiently, 'he never listens to me. He never has, and I'm not going to apologise.'

'And what if *he* does?' Roberta asked curiously, and Emily stared at her as if she had just announced that she were a fugitive from the planet Mars.

She stood up and ruffled Emily's hair playfully.

'Will you be emerging from this hiding-place for lunch?' she asked.

Emily shook her head. 'Absolutely not. Not if it means eating with Dad.'

'He'll probably be off to work.' Let's keep our fingers crossed, she thought.

'Thanks, but I'll stay put.'

Roberta looked at her gravely, her eyes twinkling. 'Well, in case you're interested, there'll be a plateful of food in the fridge,' she said, and Emily threw her a watery grin and mumbled something that sounded like thanks.

Would I have accepted this job, she wondered, shutting the door behind her, if I had known that I would have been flung into this muddled, strained situation? She tried to picture what she would be doing now if she were in England, trying to conjure up a more normal family of two parents and a toddler, and failed.

It was as if Emily and Grant had both ingrained themselves into some sub-layer of her skin, as if they had been part of her life forever.

She frowned, not liking the thought. She didn't want to become too involved with them; she especially didn't want to feel that strange *frisson* when she thought of a life without Grant Adams. The man hadn't got a thing going for him, apart from the obvious, she told herself. He wasn't kindly or gentle. She would bet a million pounds that he had never dressed up as Santa Claus and handed out presents at a Christmas party.

Although who knew what he had been like when his wife was alive?

That thought was even less to her liking. It made her feel slightly sick, in fact.

She frowned, only aware that Grant was standing at the bottom of the staircase when she almost bumped into him.

She got the impression that he had been waiting for her, but when she asked him he denied it, saying abruptly, 'Don't be ridiculous. I was on my way to the kitchen for a cup of coffee.'

'In that case, don't let me stop you,' Roberta said.

He remained where he was, his forehead furrowed in a frown.

'Did you talk to Emily?' he finally asked, in a casual voice, and Roberta nodded.

He had changed into his suit. There would be no problem about him getting to work. It had hardly snowed at all in Toronto. It had all saved itself for where they had been going.

'What did she have to say?'

'I think that's something she ought to tell you herself,' Roberta said, edging past him to get to the lounge, her heart sinking when she realised that he was following her.

Every time he was around, her damned heart seemed to take off on a different tangent. Then she had to start re-erecting her stupid defences, anxiously praying that he wouldn't knock them down with a smile or a look or a touch. God, she thought. I'm such a fool.

Why doesn't he just leave? If he was intending to go to work, why couldn't he just leave now?

'I suppose she gave you a litany of excuses,' he carried on, as if she hadn't spoken, and she rounded on him angrily.

'I have no intention of telling you what she said. It's up to you to listen to what she's got to say——'

'As I thought, she ran to you with stories about how I didn't listen to her!'

'Did you?'

'I acted in the manner I thought best,' he said, with the slightest edge of discomfort in his voice.

'In that case, you have to excuse me if I don't agree with your behaviour.'

'What . . . !' He was lost for words.

'If you're not careful, this rift between the two of you will harden, and in the years to come you'll turn around and ask yourself how it happened, but by then it'll be too late to do anything about it.'

'Philosophising again?' he mocked.

'You can do as you like,' she said, meeting his brilliant green eyes levelly, 'but if I were you I'd go up to Emily's room and talk things out with her.'

'Well, you're not,' he said flatly, and Roberta shrugged.

She had switched on the television and sat down, and he stood between her and the set, his eyes narrowed.

'Don't watch television when I'm talking to you,' he barked out.

'How can I watch anything? You're standing in front of me.'

'And spare me your wit. I just want to know what sort of state my daughter's in.'

'And as I've already said, you must go and talk to her to find out. She's in her bedroom.'

It was difficult to focus on something else when he was standing there in front of her, aggressive and disturbing. Her mind was cool, but just under the surface her emotions were soaring wildly out of control.

'I'm on my way to work,' he said, as if she hadn't noticed his clothes. 'I'm in a bit of a hurry. I have to clinch the Japanese deal today if we're to keep any sort of confidentiality in the market. It's just too sensitive, and——'

'Then you'll just have to postpone it, won't you?' Roberta murmured, and he gave her a black look, as if he had known exactly what she had been going to say but didn't like it nevertheless.

'You're damned stubborn, do you know that?' he asked softly, but his features had softened and his glance, when it fell on her, made her body go hot.

'Am I?' she asked in a strangled voice, for want of anything more intelligent to say.

'All right.' He made it sound as though they had been fighting a battle and he had been forced, to his surprise, to admit defeat. 'I'll go up and see her. I suppose it's either that or having to put up with that silent, aggravating, accusing stare of yours.' He walked towards her and she shrank back automatically in the chair. 'Don't expect me back tonight, and just remember——' he leaned towards her and Roberta fought to breathe '—there's still some unfinished business between us. See you in the morning.'

He left the room before she had time to gather her thoughts back into order, and she stared at the television set, her mind a thousand miles away.

All the confusion of the last few hours had made her think that their lovemaking had been overshadowed, that she could relax a bit on that front.

She expelled one long, shaky breath. Maybe, she thought, I should just leave, but the prospect left her with a cold feeling in the pit of her stomach.

She felt as if she was in a trap. In desperation, she switched her attention to what was happening on the television, only to find out with disgust that it was a chat show on men who could not commit themselves in a relationship.

But of course, she thought uneasily, that was hardly her problem, because she didn't want commitment anyway. She didn't want anything at all from Grant Adams, except peace of mind.

So why, a little voice said slyly, do you feel that nervous excitement whenever he's around? And why, it continued unfairly, can't you think of him without being emotionally affected?

The questions kept coming back to her for the remainder of the day, even though she busied herself around the house, cooking and doing some cleaning, and wondering how on earth Mrs Thornson coped without suffering from stress fatigue.

It really was a massive house, and after Emily's impromptu gathering the evening before all of the rooms seemed to have enough disorder in them to warrant some sort of attention.

By the end of the day, she felt physically exhausted, if nothing else.

Emily, though, she was pleased to see, had recovered from her sulks. Roberta didn't mention it and she didn't ask what Grant had said to her either, knowing that direct questioning would be a sure way to ensure total silence on the subject, but over the course of the day she gathered that, if an apology from him had not been forthcoming, then he had come as close as he ever would to one.

The gesture had been enough to lift his daughter's spirits, and Roberta had to admit that she did feel vaguely pleased that she had had some part in instigating it. Not that Grant would ever admit as such.

'So he's not the villain of the piece after all,' she said to Emily, as she was preparing to go to bed.

Emily shrugged. 'Of course, he's not like normal fathers,' she said, giving the impression that normal fathers had two heads, or four arms, 'but,' another casual shrug, 'I suppose he did make an effort, surprise, surprise. A first for him.' She glanced at Roberta coyly. 'Did you have anything to do with it?'

'Not really,' Roberta hedged, slipping under the duvet and searching about for her book. She had brought the outdated Western back with her from the log cabin, with some irritatingly stupid notion that she was morally obliged to finish it even though it brought back vivid memories of her night there.

'"Not really"? What does "not really" mean?'

'It means that it's past your bedtime.'

'You told him to come up and talk to me, didn't you?'

Roberta opened her mouth to say 'not really,' and then saw from the penetrating look in Emily's eyes that she wanted a more elaborate answer.

'I did mention that it might be a good idea,' she said awkwardly. She sincerely hoped that this would not start Emily off on another rousing lecture about her father but, to her surprise, she smiled and looked at her from under her lashes.

'Fantastic,' she said with a hint of admiration. 'Even Grandmother can't get him to do something like that.'

Roberta pulled out her book and pointedly sifted through the pages, trying to remember which particular shoot-out she had reached.

'Old age,' Roberta said lightly. 'I've heard it mellows people.'

'He's not that old.' Emily stared at her pearly finger-nails in concentration. 'In fact, I phoned Clarissa, that friend of mine, the one who was here yesterday.'

'The one being escorted down the stairs by your father?'

Emily nodded. 'She said that she was pretty shocked by Dad's behaviour—you know, all that ranting and raving. Her parents are both teachers, and pretty old. They never rant and rave.'

Roberta resisted the impulse to smile. Poor teachers. Emily made them sound like an unfortunate species of robot.

'Anyway, get this—she thought Dad was pretty cool. Can you believe that?' She broke off her inspection of her fingernails to look at Roberta. 'In fact,' she said, 'Clarissa thought Dad was really keen-looking.'

'Did she, now?' Roberta tried concentrating on her book.

'She did.' Emily nodded vigorously. 'Do you?'

'Do I what?'

'Think that Dad's good-looking.'

Roberta placed her book carefully down on her lap and folded her hands over it. 'Your father is certainly a good-looking man,' she ventured.

'Attractive?'

'Moderately.'

'Are you attracted to him?'

Roberta gave her a shocked look, and felt betraying colour flood her cheeks. 'Now, look here, young lady,' she said firmly 'it's way past your bedtime. If you don't get going, there'll be some more ranting and raving pretty soon, and I'll be the one doing it.'

Emily sprang off the bed, grinning, and left the room, slamming the door behind her with her usual lack of delicacy.

This, Roberta thought, giving up on the shoot-out, has been a long day. A long two days, in fact.

She switched off her bedside light and fell asleep almost immediately, only waking up the following morning when Emily brought her a tray of breakfast in bed.

Was this the same girl who had told her in no uncertain terms when she had first arrived that there was no way that they would ever be more than two strangers forced to live under the same roof?

Her moods were as changeable as the weather, but Roberta knew that they had forged a friendship which she hoped would last beyond the Atlantic.

They spent the day sightseeing and browsing in one of the bookstores, immodestly called The World's Largest Bookstore. Roberta noticed, with amusement, that the author of her Western was an amazingly prolific writer, with several dozen other titles to his credit, and she shared the joke with Emily.

It was an enjoyable day, spoilt only by the fact that, on their return, Grant's car was parked in the courtyard.

'You're home early, Dad,' Emily greeted him in the lounge where he was having a drink. Her voice was non-chalant enough but her cheeks were pink with delight.

He looked past her to Roberta and drawled, 'I must be getting senile. I've never had so many early evenings in years.' Then he quickly reverted his attention to his daughter, asking her about their day, his face interested as he listened.

He was a good listener. He asked questions, offered information about some of the places they intended to visit, and Roberta watched from the sidelines, hardly hearing what he was saying, only seeing the sensual cast of his features, trying to slap down her imagination which had sprung into life with a venom and was taking her down paths that made her skin burn.

She was about to excuse herself for a bath when he shot her a direct look and said, 'What are you doing tomorrow evening?'

'I beg your pardon?' Roberta answered, frantically trying to think of something she could be doing that could come in handy as an excuse, should one be needed.

'Tomorrow evening. What are you doing? Both of you?'

Was there amusement in his voice there? Roberta didn't know, but she did sigh with relief, since whatever was involved would include Emily.

'Nothing,' Emily said promptly on her behalf. 'Why?'

He drained his glass. 'Because my Japanese deal is all wrapped up. Signed, sealed and delivered, and Mr.

Ishikomo's throwing a celebration party at one of the hotels. He's asked you both along.'

'Me?' Emily frowned. 'Are you sure?'

'Quite sure, darling. He wants to meet you.' Grant looked at Roberta. 'And you, too. I think he was quite taken with you when you last met.'

'That would be nice,' she said politely. 'We'd love to come. Is it a dressy affair?'

'I haven't got anything to wear,' Emily put in. 'Can I buy something wildly expensive tomorrow?'

Grant smiled indulgently at her. 'I think I can see my way to allowing that,' he said, then he glanced at Roberta. 'And that goes for the two of you.'

'I couldn't,' Roberta said flatly.

He stared at her, his face bland. 'Couldn't? That's a word that should never exist in one's vocabulary. After all, everything's a matter of will, isn't it?' He gave her a mocking smile. 'I insist. As your employer. Buy yourself something, or I'll buy it for you.'

'I'll get it myself,' Roberta said hurriedly. Buy it for her? No, thanks. His taste probably ran to the very skimpy.

She would get herself something very understated. Something to suit the mood she wanted to project. It would be fun. In fact, the party would be fun. Emily would be there, her chaperon in a manner of speaking. And the place would be packed.

What, she thought, could be safer?

CHAPTER EIGHT

SHOPPING for something specific, Roberta discovered the following day, was a completely different matter from browsing. In the past, her clothes shopping had been highly unadventurous. A few smart outfits but, generally speaking, mostly clothes that she could comfortably wear to work. Things that could survive finger paints and baked beans and be thrown in the wash without her suffering traumatic attacks wondering whether the delicate material would be damaged by water that was too hot.

Just out of sheer habit, she had initially been drawn to affordable items in muted colours, but Emily was having nothing of that.

She had launched herself into looking for something for herself with gusto, and she demanded that Roberta do likewise.

'You look like an old maid in grey,' she had said right from the start, and Roberta had grimaced.

'I am an old maid,' she had said, amused, which had only served to stoke Emily's determination to find her something bright, adventurous and very *haute couture*.

They trailed from shop to shop, and it amazed Roberta that a teenager was more *au fait* with what was going on in the world of fashion than she was.

Did that say something about her, or about Emily? she wondered. Or maybe the simple truth was that being brought up with money did away with the constant need to compromise, which most people were forced to do.

It was hard to fight Emily's determined enthusiasm, though, and after a while Roberta allowed herself to flow with the tide.

They finally arrived back at the house laden with bags, and Roberta noted with relief that Grant was not back yet. She had felt unbearably guilty charging the dress to his account, and she had a feeling that if he so much as cross-examined her she would have no hesitation in returning everything to the store and making do with what she had in her wardrobe.

They were not due to leave until seven-thirty, and at six-thirty promptly Emily hustled her off to the bedroom like a little girl, insisting that she couldn't possibly get dressed, made up and perfumed in under an hour.

Roberta had never seen her so excited before. It was only an invitation to a dinner, but she was reacting as though she had been granted her dream of a lifetime. In a lot of ways it was rather sad. Had Grant so absented himself from his daughter's life that his sudden presence there had such a staggering effect? In one way, it was heart-warming, but in another it was vaguely dangerous, because what would happen if for some reason this fragile truce was broken?

Children needed the continued support and interest of their parents. Did Grant realise that? She frowned and began applying her make-up, taking much more care than was usual for her, accentuating her wide grey eyes, which she personally considered her best feature, with smoky black mascara.

When she finally inspected herself in the full-size mirror in the bedroom, she wondered whether she was looking at the same person. There was nothing discreet or understated about her appearance tonight at all.

The dress was seductively figure-hugging, designed to stir the imagination rather than state the obvious, and the high-heeled shoes made her look longer and slimmer than she had expected. She felt terribly glamorous. Emily's expert approval, which Roberta found highly amusing considering her age, made her laugh, but she wasn't laughing as they descended the staircase to where Grant was waiting for them both.

In fact she felt horribly shy and nervous, and it was an effort to compose her features into their usual unruffled expression.

He complimented Emily on her appearance, which made her blush even though she tried desperately to appear blasé, then he ran his eyes over Roberta, quickly at first, then more slowly, taking her in inch by leisurely inch until she felt her legs go wobbly at the lengthy inspection.

She immediately began asking him a series of questions about the venue, simply to take her mind off her self-consciousness, keeping up her prattle as they walked towards the car, trying not to react as he opened the door for her and she slipped inside, lightly brushing him in so doing.

The car glided through the streets, which had been meticulously cleared of snow, towards the hotel which was on the outskirts of the city centre.

It turned out not to be the grand, highly efficient but impersonal hotel that she was expecting, but a rather smaller place, more along the lines of some of the exquisite country inns to be found in England. There were a lot of cars parked outside, and as soon as they entered she felt herself relax in the throng of people.

Mr Ishikomo and his wife greeted them personally, and Grant introduced both of them to his colleagues, most of whom had brought their children, and after some hesitation Emily was drawn away by a girl of her own age, and vanished into the crowd.

'Just remember, Emily,' Grant said, as she was walking away. 'No drink.'

Emily looked over her shoulder at him with a cryptic smile. 'I told you, Dad, that's not my scene. Getting drunk is very un-cool.'

'You really seem to have had an effect on her,' he said, turning to Roberta and handing her a glass of champagne from the tray being passed around by the waiter. 'She seems far more settled than she was a few months ago. Mother,' he said drily, 'tries her best, but I think she finds Emily rather daunting at times.'

If she finds Emily daunting, Roberta thought, then lord knows how she finds you.

'Grandparents are in an awkward position,' she said non-committally. 'They sometimes find it difficult to lay down the law with their grandchildren. The bond is usually too much of a sympathetic one.'

He was listening to her, his head cocked slightly to one side.

'You could be right,' he agreed, staring down at her intently. 'I suppose you have quite a bit of experience of seeing that sort of thing firsthand in your job.'

'Yes, as a matter of fact, I do.'

'And tell me,' he continued lazily, 'what do you think of single-parent families?' He twirled the stem of his champagne glass and then took a deep mouthful, not taking his eyes off hers.

Roberta sipped nervously from her glass. 'It's a broad subject,' she said, wondering where exactly this line of questioning was leading.

'What do you think of Vanessa?' he asked, his swift change of subject taking her by surprise.

'I barely know the woman,' Roberta said, bewildered. 'Why do you ask?'

'I had lunch with her today. She seems eager to fill the role of my late wife, and now I think that perhaps Emily would benefit from having a mother-figure around, don't you?'

Roberta stiffened. 'I have no idea. I haven't got my crystal ball with me at the moment, so I couldn't possibly hazard a guess at how Emily would turn out if you married Vanessa.' She almost found herself choking on the words.

'But what do you think? You have got some thoughts on the matter, I take it. You seem to on every other matter.'

Roberta looked away, aware of her fingers unsteadily clutching the stem of her glass. 'I don't know,' she mumbled. 'If you're in love with her and the feeling is mutual, then——'

'Love?' His eyes held a cynical glint. 'Who's talking about love? You don't believe in all that claptrap, do you?'

Her eyes flashed angrily at him. She had thought that she was in love with Brian, had sworn afterwards that she would never love anyone again, that she would never put herself in the position of being at the mercy of someone else, but now that the question had been asked she found that, oddly enough, when she considered it, yes, she still did believe in love.

The mere acknowledgement of that scared her because she knew that she shouldn't. Love was capricious, unpredictable; it caused pain. She hadn't even loved Brian, and look at how the memory of him could still stir her to feel sullied. So what if she truly loved a man and was disappointed in her love?

Even so, for some reason, the thought of life without it suddenly seemed hollow.

'I don't know what's made you so cynical,' she responded tightly, 'but I really don't see the point of a relationship if it's to be conducted like a business affair.'

'Oh, I don't know,' he mused thoughtfully. 'Business affairs are far less taxing on the nerves than emotional flights of fancy.'

'If you say so,' Roberta responded in a clipped voice. She didn't want to pursue this conversation. She looked around the room, inordinately relieved when some of his business colleagues approached them, and even more relieved when one of them said jokingly, 'It's not fair for you to hog the prettiest girl in the room,' and led her away towards the bar. He was a young man, with a boyish, friendly face. His wife, he told her, was mulling about somewhere in the room talking girls' talk with a friend. He hated girls' talk, he confided, and he was sick of shop talk. So he asked her all about London, and Roberta obligingly made all the right responses, but her thoughts were a thousand miles away.

Still dwelling, in fact, on her conversation with Grant. Was he really planning on marrying Vanessa? He had hardly seemed besotted with her but then, as he had pointed out, that was not a necessity when it came to marriage. In fact, it was a drawback.

A while ago, he had not wanted to give the other woman any scope for setting her sights higher than a romp in bed with him, but he was beginning to see what Roberta had seen all along, and that was that Emily needed a maternal hand in her life.

Roberta finished her glass of champagne and absent-mindedly accepted a refill.

There was no point in thinking too long or too hard on what Grant Adams decided to do with his life. That wasn't her problem. In under two weeks she would be on a plane bound for Heathrow. She would be leaving all this behind, and not a minute too soon.

She tried very hard to concentrate on what Brad was saying to her. Across the room, her eyes rested on Grant, who was indolently dominating the conversation among a group of businessmen who appeared to be hanging on to his every word, and a few women who were eyeing him with blatant interest.

Emily was nowhere to be seen, though she did make a reappearance when dinner was served, a casual but elaborately concocted cold buffet meal, with everything from smoked salmon and tiger prawns to salads of every description. And, in the centre of the long table, an ice figure of two swans, their necks entwined, dominated the spread.

'Seems a shame that it's destined to become a huge puddle of water, doesn't it?' she commented to Brad and his wife, and they laughed.

It was after midnight before the party began disbanding. Roberta thought with amusement that you could always tell when people were thinking of leaving. They always began complaining about the weather and wondering aloud how long their journey home would take.

She was murmuring her goodbyes to Brad and his wife, assuring them that yes, she would take them up on their invitation to visit their sprawling house in the surburbs just whenever she wanted, really, when she heard Grant's voice from behind her and she swung around to face him.

'We seemed to have rather missed each other this evening,' he drawled, watching her.

'Don't we?' Roberta answered. 'Are you ready to leave? If so, I'll just go and get my coat. And Emily, wherever she is.'

'Come with me,' he said, taking her by the hand, and she felt her skin begin to tingle again. 'Let's have a few words with Mr Ishikomo and his wife before we go.'

Roberta nodded. She had spoken briefly to both of them in the course of the evening, but there had been too many people to hold any kind of conversation, and besides, as the hosts, they were obliged to mingle.

Emily had drifted out from one of the adjoining rooms and she now tagged along, still rather bright-eyed, and Roberta made a cryptic comment about sticking to soft drinks next time she went out, since champagne was definitely soporific.

'You old timers,' Emily teased. 'In a year's time you won't be up to going out at all. You'll just want to spend your evening whiling away your time in front of cups of cocoa.'

'Does that scenario appeal?' Grant murmured lazily in her ear.

'I can think of worse,' Roberta said lightly. 'What about you?'

'Depends who I'm whiling away my time with.'

Roberta flashed him a polite, expressionless smile. If he planned on marrying Vanessa, it didn't take a great deal of imagination to work out exactly what nature of whiling away they would be doing, and she doubted that it would involve cups of cocoa.

She tried to imagine what she would be doing in a year's time, and drew a blank.

One thing was for certain: whatever she would be doing, she would be doing it on her own. That thought, which previously had filled her with a light-headed feeling of freedom after Brian, now filled her with a vague painful numbness, and she remembered what she had said to Emily earlier on about being an old maid. Didn't it have a dreadfully lonely ring to it?

It struck her that she didn't want to end up embittered and alone. She wanted companionship, but she wanted excitement as well and, as far as she could see, the two were not compatible. Excitement, she thought, was the forte of people like Grant Adams, men that she should run from as fast as her legs would take her.

She thought back to that night in the cabin, the warmth and hunger of his caresses. Heady excitement. She felt her body squirm.

Emily was prattling on to Mr Ishikomo and his wife, talking quickly until they told her laughingly that she had to slow down if they were to understand a word of what she was saying.

'Our English,' Mrs Ishikomo said, her delicate features rueful, 'is still not so very good.'

Roberta smiled. 'It's a whole lot better than my Japanese,' she said, to which Mr Ishikomo replied,

'You must get Mr Adams here to teach you it, then!'

'I had no idea that you spoke Japanese,' she said spontaneously, turning to him, momentarily distracted from what she had been about to say, which was that he would need to be a very good teacher if he could teach her Japanese in under two weeks. Not, she thought, that he would make a very good teacher anyway. His patience wouldn't run to it.

'There are quite a few things you don't know about me,' he said, amused.

'But time enough to find out,' Mr Ishikomo said, his face beaming as he looked at them from behind his spectacles.

Roberta opened her mouth to explain that a fortnight was really not a very long time, not that she wanted to find out anyway, but he continued with evident pleasure.

'I hear about your adventure in the log cabin,' he said, still smiling. 'My wife thinks that it is all very romantic.'

Roberta's face had gone bright red. 'It was all an accident,' she stammered. 'We... Grant... he had some work to do, he needed the journey up to finish it, so I drove him up, except the snow... we were marooned; it really wasn't planned at all.' Instead of sounding clear and articulate she heard her voice dwindling pathetically into silence, and wondered why Grant wasn't saying something. After all, the whole damned episode had been entirely his fault.

'In my country,' Mr Ishikomo said, 'courtships are not conducted in quite this manner but, of course, you westerners, you do things differently.'

Mrs Ishikomo was nodding her agreement and Roberta looked at them, at a loss for words.

She darted a glance at Emily, who was grinning, enjoying the spectacle of an adult in an embarrassing position.

'I think there's been a bit of a misunderstanding here.' Roberta cleared her throat, deciding that she might as well say something since Grant was maintaining an infuriating silence.

'Darling,' she heard him whisper in her ear, 'how can you say that?' He looked at his Japanese hosts and smiled, circling Roberta with his arm and pulling her lightly towards him. 'As Roberta said, it wasn't planned. Not even I could time the weather so beautifully.' There was some amused laughter at this point, and Roberta gritted her teeth together, wondering what the hell was going on. 'But we did enjoy our little sojourn there, didn't we?'

Emily was wearing a pleased smile, as though she had somehow manoeuvred the whole thing.

'We did?' Roberta asked weakly.

'We certainly did.' Grant's voice was firm and his fingers tightened on her arm.

Mr Ishikomo adjusted his spectacles. 'Well, we are here for two weeks more before we return to Japan. We would be honoured if you would be our guests at a friend's house. It is on a lake, and very charming.'

'We'd love to,' Grant accepted, his fingers tightening a little more on her arm.

'I fix a date with you when I see you tomorrow.'

As soon as they were back in the car Emily began with a tirade of questions, none of which Roberta answered. She had a feeling that if she attempted any form of speech just yet, the result would be an unintelligible croak.

She stared out of the window, listening to Grant's smooth, persuasive voice, and as soon as they got home she said to Emily in as normal a voice as she could muster, 'You must be off to bed now. I'll see you in the morning.'

'But...' Emily protested, then her face creased into an impulsive smile. 'I guess I'll have to listen to you from now on.'

Roberta said something inoffensive and vague, and as soon as Emily had vanished out of sight she turned to Grant fiercely.

'I want a word with you,' she hissed. 'Now!'

Grant looked anything but daunted by her tone of voice. If anything, there was amusement in his eyes, and that only infuriated her further.

She stalked off towards the lounge and sat down on one of the chairs, her lips pursed as he strolled into the room without any apparent haste.

'What's going on?' she burst out furiously. 'How could you let Mr Ishikomo and his wife think that we...that we...' Her words ended in spluttered incoherence.

'You're in quite a state,' he said lazily, standing up. 'Would you care for a drink? It might soothe your nerves.'

He walked across to the bar and poured himself a glass of brandy, taking his time, standing by the bar and looking at her over the rim of his glass as he took a mouthful of the liquid.

'I am not in a state!' Roberta said in a high voice. 'And I do not want a drink. What I want is an explanation. Why didn't you tell Mr Ishikomo that he was on the wrong track? Why didn't you tell him that there's nothing between us?'

'There is, though, isn't there?' Grant returned silkily. 'Some very good sex, for one thing.'

'We've been through that,' she said through gritted teeth. 'I've told you that it was a mistake. In fact,' she lied, 'I'd completely forgotten about it.'

Grant looked at her disbelievingly, and Roberta felt the blood rush to her head. The arrogance of the man, the conceit! He must be damned certain of his sexual charisma to stand there and tell her that he had made any kind of lasting impression on her. The fact that he had made her even angrier.

'This is all beside the point!' she shouted. 'You still haven't answered my question!'

He prowled around the room for a moment and Roberta followed him with her eyes, angry at his behaviour and at the fact that even now, at the very height of her rage, his body was still sending out messages that her own found it impossible to ignore.

He had shed his dinner-jacket in the hall, and his crisp white shirt moulded the broad width of his shoulders, reminding her with sickening clarity of that hard, bronzed torso that had sent her senses swimming.

She tore her gaze away from him and reminded him coldly that she was still waiting for his answer.

Finally he sat down on the chair opposite hers, stretching out his long legs on the coffee-table in front of him.

'It was convenient,' he said succinctly, and she stared at him in complete bewilderment.

'I don't follow you.'

'Mr Ishikomo, as I said, is unused to our western customs——'

'*Your* western customs,' she corrected, knowing exactly to what he was referring.

He shrugged as if the distinction didn't really matter, and swallowed some more of his drink. 'Whatever. The fact is that he incorrectly assumed that we were slightly more involved than we are.'

'Slightly more involved? Isn't that a bit of an understatement?'

'So it is,' Grant agreed. 'I must be picking that up from you.'

'You could have put him straight,' Roberta informed him, more in control of herself now and determined not to give in to another explosive burst of anger. 'You could have told him the truth.'

'That we made love?'

'No!' she snapped. 'All I'm saying is that you didn't have to encourage him in his bizarre ideas about us.'

'I told you, it was convenient. There are still a few more signatures needed on that deal.'

'I see,' Roberta said tightly. 'You didn't want him to renege on it because he found your behaviour offensive to his principles.'

'Something like that.'

'That's despicable. And what about Emily? How are you going to explain all this to her?'

Grant stared at her blankly, as though he didn't foresee any problems there at all. 'She'll understand,' he said at last. 'She's a big girl now.'

Roberta sighed impatiently. 'I don't appreciate being used,' she said with considerable restraint. 'What you did was unnecessary. I'm sure Mr Ishikomo would have signed whatever he needed to sign without your committing me to some stupid, phoney relationship. Besides, what about your marriage plans to Vanessa?' she threw in as an afterthought. 'I thought you were slotting her in the role of surrogate mother for Emily?'

'That was hypothetical,' Grant said, averting his eyes. 'She wouldn't fit the bill at all, as a matter of fact.' A dull red flush darkened his cheeks, and Roberta stared at him with dawning comprehension.

'I was convenient in more than one way, wasn't I?' she asked. 'You wanted an excuse for getting Vanessa off your back, and what better than to inform her that you and I were involved in a relationship?'

He didn't deny it, and she could have thrown something at him.

'Well, I'm not in the market for exploitation!' She stood up, shaking with anger, but before she could leave the room he had crossed the space between them, his dark eyebrows meeting in a frown.

'I'm sorry,' he muttered, and when she turned away he forced her back to look at him, holding her chin in between his fingers so that she had no option but to meet his eyes.

'I didn't think that you would react so violently. I have to admit that I acted without thinking.' It was as much of an apology as she was ever likely to get out of him, but it wasn't enough.

That's the problem with you, she thought, you just don't think. He had made love to her at the cabin, initially because she brought back to him memories of the woman he had loved, and then to satisfy his passing curiosity. He would quite happily have a two-week relationship with her, if only to meet what he considered the challenge of making her abandon her high-sounding principles.

He didn't care about her. She was a world apart from his life, as foreign to him as if she lived on another planet instead of in another country.

It didn't cross his mind that he had the power to hurt her. It was the first time she had admitted as much without sugar-coating it in a jumble of reasons why that couldn't possibly happen. The raw truth of it was, she now realised, that, in spite of everything, she had allowed herself to be put in a situation from which she could emerge a catastrophic loser.

She felt the tears of self-pity stinging her eyelids and she blinked rapidly. This was so different, wasn't it? Nothing like Brian. Because she hadn't loved Brian, had she? Infatuation for a while, yes. But never love. She knew now, because *this* was love. This irrational, intense feeling she had for Grant Adams was love. She was hopelessly, stupidly in love with him.

'I thought you would see it as a harmless and temporary bit of subterfuge.'

'I hate you, Grant Adams.'

A frown of displeasure crossed his handsome face.

'You're self-centred and arrogant, and you have no idea how to treat people!' There was a lot more she could say on the subject, but the words refused to come out. They remained locked inside her head.

'You're over-reacting,' he muttered.

'I am not over-reacting. I don't suppose anyone has ever told you this before, but you don't think twice about taking advantage of women, do you? You go through life using people to suit your own ends. You men are all the bloody same!'

He was wearing an unreadable expression when he looked at her. 'That's a bit of a generalisation, isn't it?' he murmured softly, his green eyes piercing into hers intently, and she burst out in a rush,

'Is it? Is it really? Not from what I can see! You wanted to know about Brian. Well, I'll tell you, he used me.' There was self-disgust and bitterness in her voice. 'He made wild promises of love; he would have promised the moon if it had been within his grasp, but of course it was all a ploy. He wanted something from me all right, but it wasn't love and friendship.'

'Carry on,' Grant said urgently.

'So that you can have a good laugh at my expense?' Roberta jeered, her jaw aching from the effort of withholding her tears.

'That's one sin I'm not guilty of,' he said roughly, forcing her to look at him when all she wanted to do was to look away.

Now that she had started, she had a burning, compulsive desire to get it all off her chest. Confession cleansed, and there was no one she had spoken to before about Brian. When her friends in London had asked, she had assumed a smiling, rueful demeanour and shrugged her shoulders philosophically.

'He... My mother had recently died, you see. We were very close, just the opposite of you and Emily.' She took a deep breath and ventured a smile. 'I was a bit of an emotional wreck at the time, and he came along. Compliments, flowers and good wine. The sort of stuff that bowls girls over, but I had always thought that I would never be caught by that trap. But I was. He was good-looking, and I guess he picked me up when I was down and I clung to him, totally blind to what was really going on. Pathetic, isn't it?'

Grant didn't answer, and she wondered what he was thinking. If he was laughing at her, then he certainly didn't show it.

'I had been left some money by Mum. Not a massive amount, but enough to keep me going for quite a while if I invested it properly.' Her voice was calm now, not hysterical at all. 'He knew that from the very start. It was no secret. Who knows, maybe he was genuinely attracted to me to begin with, before he decided that I was better suited as a meal-ticket than a prospective wife.'

Grant knew what was coming. She could see it on his face.

'Need I carry on?' she asked him unsteadily. 'He persuaded me out of my money and I stupidly let him. So, you see, I'm not just a prim school-ma'am type, I'm a foolish prim school-ma'am type.'

Grant clicked his tongue impatiently. 'My description of you was out of line. And untrue, anyway.'

She couldn't bear his sympathy. Sympathy always rubbed shoulders with pity, and pity was something she could do without.

She fidgeted to escape his grip and his fingers tightened on her arms.

'I'm not like him,' he said tightly. 'Look at me! Do you see me as being cast in the same mould?'

Roberta looked at him, and her heart gave a little uncomfortable leap. There was a depth and intelligence to him, a sense of humour, that had all been absent from Brian, but there was no way that she was going to admit as much. There was no way that she was going to let him know how vulnerable she was to him.

He was incapable of love, just like Brian had been. The unbidden thought surged through her and she felt a quiver of panic.

Wasn't that the crux of it? She wanted his love, however fiercely she had tried to deny it to herself. Not safety, control over her life. She could do without those. What she needed was his love, and that was the one thing he could never give her, or anyone else. He was locked in his past and she, for one, did not possess the key to release him.

She jerked out of his grip and took a shaky step backwards.

'I'm going up to bed now,' she muttered, more sharply than she had intended.

'Stay down here. Talk to me,' he said harshly, and she shook her head.

'What else is there to talk about? I just don't like being used. If I over-reacted, as you put it, then I'm sorry, but I don't approve of men who exploit women and, as you can see, I speak from experience.'

She turned away abruptly and walked towards the door, half expecting him to try and stop her, but he didn't. He remained where he was, and as soon as she was out of the room Roberta ran all the way up to her bedroom and locked the door.

All sorts of thoughts were running through her head, all sorts of agonising questions, and she didn't want to address any of them. It was all pointless, anyway.

Time would answer them; time would cure this painful, confused ache in her heart.

CHAPTER NINE

IN THAT pleasant limbo halfway between asleep and awake Roberta lay in bed, knowing vaguely that there was a reason why she did not want to get up.

As soon as she opened her eyes, it all came rushing back like a dreadful nightmare. Mr Ishikomo, his assumptions, Grant's arrogant exploitation of the situation because it suited him. Oh, God. Emily. She closed her eyes and wondered if she could somehow contrive to spend the remainder of her stay in Toronto in bed, preferably with laryngitis, because the consequences of what had happened the night before were too awful to think about.

Emily did not give her the option. She had hardly sat down in the lounge to begin reading the newspaper when she rushed in, a tornado of excitement, brimming over with all the expected questions, and Roberta smiled weakly, waiting until Emily had finished, then she said hopefully, 'I have the most dreadful headache.'

Emily frowned petulantly. 'How can you have a headache? All of this is so exciting! I never suspected a thing,' she carried on admiringly. 'Some dark horse, you are.'

Roberta eyed her warily, wondering whether she could try and explain everything, but one look at her excited face squashed all her good intentions.

Besides, why should she do the explaining? Grant would have to do that. He had got them both into this mess and and, as far as she was concerned, he could damned well get them out of it.

But that didn't help. As she and Emily browsed in Kensington Market, she found that she couldn't distance herself from what had happened. She couldn't just shove it to the back of her mind, ignore Emily's questions, and philosophically wait for Grant to extricate them from the catastrophe.

She smiled, dodged, evaded and ended up back at the house later on with the screaming headache that she had feebly complained about earlier in the morning.

It's not my problem, she kept telling herself. I'm only a visitor here, I'll be off and out of all this soon. But she found it impossible to look at Emily and pretend that it would all be forgotten as soon as she left Toronto.

By the time Emily retired upstairs for her bath, Roberta felt as though she had been subjected to an ordeal about as gruelling as the Chinese water torture.

She sat down on one of the sofas in the lounge and closed her eyes, wishing that she could fall asleep and wake up to discover that it had all been a bad dream.

In fact, she was very nearly falling asleep through sheer mental exhaustion when she heard the doorbell, and she wearily got to her feet, in no particular haste to find out who was at the door.

She had a sneaking suspicion that whoever it was would be bringing bad news. Wasn't that just typical of life? It was never content to throw just one obstacle in front of you; it always threw a series of them, until the light at the end of the tunnel became so obscure that you just wanted to give up halfway through and admit defeat.

She opened the door, and sighed when she saw who was there. Vanessa. Long, blonde, wrapped in a huge beige cashmere coat, and wearing an expression that was distinctly unpleasant.

Roberta padded back to the lounge, with Vanessa following in her wake, and sat down, waiting to see what line of questioning was about to come, because one thing was for certain: the other woman had not visited to offer her congratulations and enjoy a jovial cup of tea.

Roberta tucked her legs under her, waiting for Vanessa to speak, and thought, When you get back from work, Grant Adams, I'm going to kill you.

'So you won.' The blonde came to the point without procrastinating. She had removed her coat, and she sat gracefully on the chair, her legs crossed. The high, childlike voice was acid, and Roberta said evasively, 'I didn't think it had been a battle.' So Grant had told her, she thought.

Vanessa looked at her expressionlessly. 'I would never have thought that you would be the one he would decide to settle down with. He had his choice of women. Why you?'

Roberta felt her hackles rise and she thought, Wonderful, what a line in compliments! But she had no intention of becoming embroiled in a fruitless argument over a fictitious situation. She smiled politely and looked blank, as though she couldn't quite follow what Vanessa was getting at, and didn't much care anyway.

'I know I should be a graceful loser,' Vanessa said, twirling her fingers in her lap and looking rather piteous, 'but I fought hard for him.'

'Maybe you fought a bit too hard,' Roberta said sympathetically, and the other woman nodded.

'Maybe I did. Maybe if I had held out a bit more, played hard to get a bit longer, he wouldn't have lost interest.'

Maybe, Roberta wanted to tell her, you should look at it along the lines of having had a narrow escape, but she bit back the words. Vanessa's disappointment was another by-product of Grant's arrogance, and he could get himself out of it as well.

'I don't think I could have coped with Emily, anyway,' Vanessa was saying. 'She's terribly difficult and we rub each other up the wrong way.' She paused, and Roberta knew that she was considering her position of jilted lover, working out how she could get out of it with some semblance of pride. 'The fact is, it would probably never have worked between Grant and me. I would have been fighting a battle with that child all the time.'

'Very tiring,' Roberta murmured vaguely.

Vanessa nodded vehemently and began to look slightly less piteous. 'Very. Come to think of it, if he hadn't called the whole thing off, I probably would have. I mean, he's sexy as hell and rich with it, but that's not all there is to life, is it?'

'Definitely not,' Roberta agreed.

'I can see you understand what I'm saying,' Vanessa informed her, confident now. 'Well, you can tell Grant Adams from me that I'm well shot of him! Good riddance.' She stood up and Roberta followed suit, following her to the front door.

'I'll tell him,' she promised, and she would, too, along with lots of other things which would be of a slightly more unpleasant nature.

Vanessa slipped on her coat and said warmly, 'I'm glad we had this little chat. I must admit that I was feeling a little angry when I first showed up here, but I'm not now. And I'll tell you something else,' she added, glancing up the stairs to make sure that Emily was nowhere around. 'It might seem a bed of roses to you now, but watch out. Whatever he's told you, he's incapable of love.'

'Is he?' Roberta tried to look startled and failed.

'He is. He never talks about his wife, but he once said that she was the reason that he would never make the mistake of loving anyone again.'

'Did he?' Roberta asked with interest now, and Vanessa nodded.

'I don't envy you your lot,' she said, magnanimous in her loss, now that she had reasoned it all out for herself and decided that she could re-write the episode in slightly different hues. 'Good luck.'

Luck, she thought acidly. That's something Grant Adams is going to need when he walks through that front door. Luck to be alive when I'm through with him. If things had seemed black the night before, they seemed even blacker now.

She had a light supper with Emily, her resentment growing with every minute, and she was positively vibrating with it as she sat watching television later that night, counting the minutes until she heard the front door.

When she finally heard it click open her body tensed and she clenched her fists on her lap. She knew that he would come in here for a nightcap; she had become accustomed to his habits. And he did.

'You're still up,' he said, shrugging himself out of his jacket and rolling up the sleeves of his shirt to expose his brown wrists, flecked with fine dark hair. She sat and watched him, simmering with anger as he poured himself a drink, wondering how he could look so damned composed when she felt so totally out of control.

'You told Vanessa that we were going to be married, didn't you?' she bit out accusingly. He had sat down next to her on the sofa, one arm stretched along the back so that it was very nearly touching her, and she wondered if he had done that on purpose. Did he know how much it was disconcerting her?

'Not in so many words,' he said lazily.

'But enough so that she got the general idea?'

He didn't say anything and Roberta bristled angrily. 'I had a little visit from her this evening,' she snapped, 'and she's asked me to tell you that you did her a favour, that she feels she's well rid of you!'

'Good.'

'Good?' Roberta repeated, thrown off course by his response. 'Good?'

He gave her a sidelong look. 'She's angry, but that's far more healthy than being hurt. Now she can forget that I ever existed, put me down to a bad experience and carry on her life without being burdened by regrets and resentment. Those are emotions that fester.'

'Are you trying to tell me something?' Roberta asked tersely, knowing that she was being distracted from what she really wanted to say, but unable to respond in any other manner. Just being so close to him muddled her. She found that she was too busy trying to avoid touching him to think clearly, and all the things that she had planned to say, which she had rehearsed so carefully earlier on, became shadowy and intangible and infinitely difficult to put into words.

'He was a bastard, but you've let it jaundice you.'

'Oh, that's rich, coming from you,' Roberta broke out. 'Are you trying to tell me that your wife didn't have a similar effect on you? You can make love, all right, you can have your affairs and pretend that that's all you want out of life, but you can't go beyond that, can you?'

His mouth hardened. 'It's a whole lot further than you can go,' he muttered.

Roberta didn't want to talk about this. 'And what about Emily?' she asked, changing the subject away from her. She looked at him and had an insane desire to put her hands against his chest, to feel the hard, lean plateau of his torso. She licked her lips nervously, alarmed at the strength of the sensation.

'Did you explain it to her?'

'No! That's up to you to do!'

'Then why are you so worked up about it? It's not your problem, is it?'

That was precisely what she had thought, but the mere fact that he could be so cool about it just added to her anger.

'I don't like deceit,' she muttered. 'I happen to be very fond of your daughter,' she carried on unsteadily. 'How is she going to feel when she discovers the truth?'

He looked at her for a long time, until the silence in the room became deafening, then he said mildly, 'We could always remedy that situation, you know.'

Roberta stared blankly at him. 'How?'

'We could always get married.'

She felt the room begin to spin. Had she heard correctly? 'I beg your pardon?' she said in a high whisper.

'I said,' he repeated patiently, taking another mouthful from his drink, 'we could always get married.'

For a minute, she glimpsed a vision of bliss, then the shutters of reality snapped down.

'A business proposition,' she said in a dull voice and, when he didn't reply, she carried on in the same flat tone. 'I'm sorry to disappoint you, but I'm not in the market for that nature of business proposition.'

'Why not?' he asked coolly. 'I can think of a lot worse. You'll have money, Emily will be happy and, face it, it's hardly as though there isn't a strong mutual attraction between us.'

'That's not the point!' Roberta protested fiercely, but she could see the way his mind was working all too clearly. She might have told him that she believed in love, but everything else she had said, everything she did, indicated just the opposite.

Why should she be so surprised at his cold, calculated proposal? A wife suited him at this present moment in time. Emily needed the stability, apart from anything else. That much he had come to realise. And she fitted the bill; it was as simple as that.

He could not give love, and he assumed the same of her. It would be a marriage unhampered by any such emotion.

Her reaction hardly surprised her. She could never accept a marriage in which she would always be the vulnerable one.

He had no love to give, and she foolishly could not consider any sort of life with him without it.

If I wasn't in love with him, she thought sickly, I would be able to see the logic of everything he was saying, might even be persuaded by it.

He was looking at her, trying to get inside her head with those brilliant eyes of his, and she muttered icily, 'You can find another suitable companion, Mr Adams. Marriage to you is definitely not in my job description.'

A shutter snapped down over his eyes and he shrugged. 'In that case, you can explain to Mr Ishikomo that his invitation for Thursday night is out of the question.'

'That's not fair!' Roberta cried out.

'And you can also explain to Emily that you have decided that you can't marry me,' he continued ruthlessly.

Tears stung the back of her eyes. 'You can't mean that! You've got to tell her yourself. She's your daughter, and that's your responsibility!'

He gave a dry, humourless laugh. 'What you mean is you want to avoid an unpleasant scene. Well, I'll explain it to her all right, but,' and he rummaged in his pockets for a business card which he tossed at her, 'Mr Ishikomo is your baby. They've already ordered the chef in for the weekend. Mrs Ishikomo is at the house getting it ready herself. So you can handle that.'

Roberta picked up the card and stared down at it miserably. 'All right, we'll go,' she whispered. 'I'll continue this farce until I leave for London. You can get your deal signed, and what you choose to do after that is your business.'

Her voice was barely audible. She didn't know how it had happened, but she had been made to feel the guilty party in this terrible affair. He had cleverly turned the tables around so the sour taste was in her mouth.

She stood up and he remained where he was, his face expressionless.

'You're a bastard,' she said shakily, and he bared his teeth in the mimicry of a smile.

'And you're a fool. I hope you spend the night thinking about the lonely little life waiting for you back in England. It might be a salutary experience.'

She turned away, almost tripping in her haste to leave the room.

She had meant what she had said to him. He was a bastard, but it made her sick to think that that was not how Emily would see it. She, Roberta, would be the focus for all that childish disillusionment and hurt and, even though she would not be around to witness it, it still hurt badly.

How was it with that man that whatever hand he had been dealt, he still managed to win?

It was ages before she finally fell asleep, and then it was only because her body could no longer remain awake.

The next few days proved even harder than she had imagined. Grant had not spoken to Emily, for which she was deeply grateful, admitting with a rueful cowardice that she could not have handled the resultant reaction with aplomb. On the other hand, it became progressively more wearing coping with the lie, and by the time Thursday finally rolled around she was almost relieved to be getting out of the house for three days.

Mrs Thornson had reappeared on Monday after her week off doing the decorating, confiding in Roberta that it had been a complete waste of time anyway, since her husband had lethargically begun the wallpapering, only to lose interest halfway through, leaving a trail of unfinished rooms behind him.

'He lacks stamina, that man,' she had said with her usual plaintive tone and economy of language. 'Needs prodding.'

Roberta had nodded sympathetically, her mind conjuring up images of rooms half-papered while the furniture stood forlornly in odd places, covered with protective sheets.

'And you'd better be good,' she told Emily, as she packed her bag. 'No wild parties.'

'With Mrs Thornson around?' Emily scoffed. 'Not likely. Anyway, I don't think I could face another scene like the last one. Although,' she added with wicked satisfaction, 'Dad would probably be in a more mellow mood with you around.'

Don't bank on it, Roberta wanted to say. She had seen very little of him recently, and what she had seen had definitely been lacking in charm.

She carried her bag downstairs to where he was waiting in the hall, tapping his keys on the stair banister, and mentally steeled herself for the drive ahead.

She had had time to think about the shocking realisation that she was in love with him, time to work out that her best method of dealing with the threat he posed was to be as polite and as distant with him as was humanly possible.

Even so, as she looked at him standing there, casually dressed in deep green trousers and a thick off-white jumper, she had to fight the alarming prickle of awareness that shot through her.

Emily was delighted that they were going away together. She had got it into her head that it was something along the lines of a naughty weekend, even though Roberta had tried to explain to her, very firmly, that it was nothing of the sort.

When Roberta turned to say goodbye, Emily threw her thin arms around her and then said playfully, 'See you in a couple of days' time, Mum!'

Grant was standing a few feet away, idly looking at his car, impatient to get going. In fact, Roberta would have said that his mind was miles away, probably on his next conquest if his past history was anything to go by, but it wasn't.

At Emily's teasing expression of fondness, he turned around swiftly, and said with hard anger, 'She's not your mother, Emily. Don't ever forget that.'

There was an uncomfortable silence, then Emily's face took on that sullen expression that Roberta had not seen for quite a while.

'It was a joke, Dad,' she said, her fists clenched. 'Where's your sense of humour? Did you decide to leave it at work today?'

'And don't you use that tone of voice on me, my girl,' he snapped, frowning.

Roberta rested her hand affectionately on the girl's shoulder and said gently, 'You run along inside. It's freezing here. I'll call you as soon as we get to Mr Ishikomo's place, all right?'

Emily nodded, but Roberta could see that Grant's abruptness with her had upset her. She was still too insecure in her relationship with her father to accept his bad moods as things that would eventually blow over. She couldn't fall back on the certainty that he loved her, whatever he might say, because, even though he did, he had in the past lacked a means of expressing it.

Roberta had thought about this, and had come to the conclusion that his wife's death had something to do with that. Maybe Emily reminded him too forcibly of lost love. Whatever, it wasn't fair of him to expect the child to obediently tune in to his mood swings without reacting.

As soon as she was in the car, Roberta said as much. 'That was a bit unnecessary, wasn't it? Telling her off like that for no apparent reason.'

'No apparent reason to you, you mean,' he responded coolly, and she stared at his hard profile, willing herself to be as aloof as he was.

'Fair enough,' Roberta said shrugging, and she let the conversation slide, looking through the car window at

the striking city skyline, then at the more sweeping land-
scape around her as they left the city behind.

Neither was speaking very much, but it was not a
comfortable silence, and as the miles slipped past she
began to wish that she had got up the courage after all
to decline Mr Ishikomo's invitation. The embarrassment would at least have been short-lived, instead
of which she now faced days of discomfort with Grant.

In the end, just to combat the silence stretched taut
between them, she began asking him about his deal with
Mr Ishikomo, about the countryside, about anything that
would lessen the atmosphere of tension. He replied
tonelessly in monosyllables, until she finally burst out,
'You're determined to make me suffer, aren't you? You
want to make my last few days here as unpleasant as
possible, don't you? Just because I turned down your
business arrangement!' She could not bring herself to
refer to it as anything else. 'Did I damage that huge ego
of yours?' she mocked. 'Are you piqued because, for
once, you didn't get your own way?'

They were driving along a quite deserted stretch of
country road now, and he suddenly swerved off on to
the snow-encrusted verge, killing the engine and then
turning to face her, his expression grim.

Her eyes widened in alarm. She had gone too far, she
could see that now, but it was too late to retract what
she had said, and she stared at him silently.

'Listen to me, lady,' he bit out in a razor-sharp voice.
'It would take more than you to have any effect on me
whatsoever. The fact of the matter is that you make me
sick. In a way, it would have been better if you were the
gold-digger I first imagined you to be, because at least
then you would be up front. No, you disgust me, because all I can see is a repressed, twisted woman, handy

with sarcasm but not much else. Sure, I offered you a deal, and you turned me down. Fair enough, but what really sticks in my throat is that you turned me down because you're nothing more than a coward who's scared witless about taking control of her life.'

'I'm in perfect control of my life!' Roberta flared back.

'Is that why we're on our way up to see Mr Ishikomo and his wife? Face it: you didn't have the guts to tell them the truth.'

'That was up to you!' Her face was flushed with miserable confusion and hurt anger.

'I bet that's how you spent your life,' he threw at her scornfully, 'letting other people make the decisions for you, happy to ride along just so long as you didn't have to take responsibility for anything.'

'That's not true,' Roberta whispered, but wasn't it? It might not have been the absolute truth, but there was enough in what he said to fill her with a giddy sense of unreality.

Hadn't her mother always made the decisions? Even her job was one in which she ultimately never had to make any hard choices. She had been a caretaker of other people's children, rather than a mother with the harsh responsibility of her own. She had been swept along by Brian until that tidal wave came crashing down around her ears.

'But I'm close, aren't I?' he said grimly. 'Well, you wear your smile when we reach that house, but when we're together don't try and pretend that you're anything other than what you are. You couldn't even handle yourself after we had made love, could you? You found it safer to hide behind it as a mistake. I'm surprised you didn't try to persuade yourself that I had seduced you. That would be your style.'

She didn't want to hear any more of this. He had said enough, and inside she was being torn in two, because he was right, but what he couldn't see was that this time she *had* made a decision. She had decided not to marry him because she was in love with him, and it was a hopeless love. But how could she tell him that?

'I'm sorry if you think that,' she said on a whisper.

'Are you really?' His voice was laced with sarcasm. 'How big of you.'

He started up the engine and it purred into life, then he pulled out into the road and Roberta closed her eyes.

Two hours later, when she next opened them, the car was pulling up outside a small house nestled amid a forest of conifer trees and overlooking the vast, flat black expanse of a lake.

She must have fallen asleep, against all odds. Maybe her body had decided to shut down temporarily because it could not cope with any more.

Whatever, she warily eyed Grant from under her lashes, wondering whether he would resume his attack on her, but he didn't. His face was expressionless as he lifted their bags out of the boot, and he barely glanced in her direction when Mr Ishikomo and his wife emerged smiling from inside the house, fussing over them like two mother hens, ushering them inside where an open fire was burning.

This place was bigger than Grant's cabin had been, less of a hideaway and more of a second home. It was tastefully furnished in rich, deep colours which gave it a warm, intimate feel, and there were shelves of books on one of the walls, not just one inadequate Western stuffed into a drawer somewhere.

She tried to feel pleased, but simply felt nostalgic, and then told herself that she was a fool to even let herself dwell on Grant Adams and his damned cabin at all.

The Japanese couple proved the perfect hosts. Perfect as far as Roberta was concerned, anyway, because they were always around, chatting, involving her in what the chef, who was a personal friend of theirs, was doing. That left her very little time alone with Grant, and for that she was grateful.

They took a long, refreshing walk around the lake, had drinks before dinner, and then ate an exquisite ten-course Japanese meal, and all the while Grant maintained his easy, assured conversation. No one would ever have guessed that he wasn't as charming to her in private as he appeared to be in public.

But she knew. She could see the impenetrable ice in his eyes where their hosts could not, and she could hear the lurking coolness in his voice when he addressed her. He had said his piece and he had nothing left to add. That was the impression that she got.

It was after midnight when Mrs Ishikomo correctly interpreted Roberta's stifled yawn as weariness, and she stood up with a smile.

'You are sleepy. We all are. Cold weather can be as tiring as hot. Let me show you to your bedroom.' Roberta obediently followed her hostess to a large double room, and was about to say goodnight when Mrs Ishikomo said coyly, 'You are in the same room, you two. Mr Ishikomo says that I must follow your more liberated tradition over here between engaged couples.'

Roberta's mouth dropped open in dismay, then she said quickly, 'Of course you don't. I'm happy to sleep in a different bedroom.' She saw Grant's mouth twist into a cynical, knowing smile, and she carried on resolutely, 'I wouldn't want to offend you. In fact, I think your way of doing things is very good, in fact——'

'No,' Mrs Ishikomo said with a smile.

'No?'

'No. You two have a good night and we will see you in the morning.' She gave a half-bow, which Grant returned, and quietly left the bedroom.

'Relax,' he said to her the minute Mrs Ishikomo was out of the room. 'I have no intention of jumping on you.' The charming mask which he had worn all afternoon was gone, and in its place was the hard expression which she had seen in the car on the drive up. 'I'll sleep on the floor.'

'Fine.' Her voice was as clipped as his was, and she watched silently as he removed his pillows and a blanket from the bed and carelessly tossed them on to the floor. She wasn't going to argue with his decision. In fact, she would have suggested it if he hadn't.

She got undressed in the bathroom, and by the time she re-emerged he was lying on the floor, his broad shoulders exposed over the blanket. Roberta switched off the light and waited for sleep. But none came. She had slept on the journey and now she was paying the price. She stared into the darkness, her eyes gradually adjusting until she could easily make out his form on the ground. And she looked at him. Without the distraction of other people around, she faced the frightening truth that, despite everything she had said, despite all her resolutions, she still wanted him. She looked at him on the floor and a desperate craving began to consume her until it filled every inch of her body.

She shoved aside her duvet and slipped out of the bed, tiptoeing across to where he was sleeping. Only to look at him, she told herself, only to appease some of this dreadful ache she felt inside.

He looked terribly peaceful lying there. Sleep softened the hard angles of his face and made him look less forbidding.

She bent a little closer and then his eyes opened. Roberta shot back in surprise.

'I...I...' she stammered in confusion.

'Was just passing so you thought you'd look me up?' He propped himself up by one elbow and surveyed her. 'Or maybe you were on your way to the bathroom?'

'Yes,' she said quickly, 'that's it. I was on my way to the bathroom.' She began to stand up, and his hand flicked out, catching her by the wrist.

'Funny sort of position to adopt for someone on their way to the bathroom, isn't it?' he asked softly.

She could feel her cheeks burning, but what could she say?

'It's very flattering to be subjected to this little appraisal of yours,' he continued in the same smooth voice, 'but I'm a little surprised after everything you've said to me. Or maybe you want to indulge in another huge mistake?'

Roberta was trembling in panic and sheer humiliation.

'Cat got your tongue?' he demanded roughly, pulling her forward towards him so that her hair flew across her face. 'Admit it, you wanted me to wake up, you wanted me to catch you staring at me, you want to make love to me.'

'No!' she protested frantically. 'That's not it at all!'

'Isn't it?' He released her and lay back down, his hands behind his head, staring upwards at the ceiling. 'Fine. Off you go to the bathroom, then.'

Roberta remained where she was. Her heart was thumping so loudly that she could hardly breathe. Her mind, which had become sluggish with panic, now shut down completely, and her body took over.

'All right, I want you,' she said huskily. With unsteady fingers she unbuttoned the front of her nightgown and he stared at her, then with a low groan he pulled her on to him, his hand seeking and finding the warmth of her breasts.

'Are you trying to drive me crazy?' he moaned, and before she could answer that one his mouth met hers in a hard, urgent kiss. The force of the kiss pressed her down against the floor, and the job of undressing, which she had started, he completed, until her nightdress lay in a heap next to her.

He pushed open her legs with his thigh and she gasped as she felt his hand move to explore the moistness between them. There was something shocking and inevitable about what they were doing. It was as if a part of her had known all along that his lean, hard body was just too irresistible.

She caressed his back, arching to allow his mouth access to the swollen tips of her nipples, then her hand cupped the back of his head, her fingers clutching the dark mass of his hair, pressing him to suckle even harder on her breasts.

Her breathing was coming in short bursts, as was his. She could feel him stiff and hot against her and, as if sensing her need, he entered her with a low cry of excitement.

She closed her eyes and her body responded to his fierce rhythm, until their release was simultaneous and explosive.

'So glad you were passing,' he murmured into her ear, 'or whatever.'

Roberta couldn't say anything. She was horrified at what she had done, horrified that her body could let her down with such monumental ease. There was no point even saying to him that it had been another mistake. Mistakes happened once.

He caressed her breast and she felt him stir against her.

'Please,' she whispered, 'not again. Not just yet. I'm awfully sleepy.'

She could feel his green eyes on her face, surprised.

'I must be losing my touch,' he murmured, and she thought, Oh, no, you're not losing your touch, I'm losing my mind.

She didn't dare speak. She didn't want him to hear the bitterness in her voice, bitterness at herself for her own pathetic fallibility. She just wanted him to fall asleep.

'Do you mind if I get back into bed?' she whispered, trying to sound normal.

'Only if I get back in it with you.'

There was no excuse for denying him that. Not now. She nodded mutely, and their two naked bodies entwined under the duvet. With small, gradual and very gentle movements, she extricated herself from his grasp.

CHAPTER TEN

LONDON felt almost humid after Toronto. The skies were grey and overcast, the rain half-heartedly splattering down, grimly reminding everyone that this was winter, after all, so what else did they expect?

Roberta sat back in the black taxi and closed her eyes for the first time since she had left Toronto.

It had been a flight of panic. She had waited until she was quite sure that Grant was asleep, then she had sneaked out of the house like a criminal, clutching his car keys, looking over her shoulder every minute, praying that her luck would hold. And it had. Fate for once had placed no obstacles in her path. In fact, it had urged her along, making sure that she did not get lost in the great, bitter Canadian blackness, turning all the traffic lights to green to speed up her escape.

In the end, though, it had been a bit of a wasted journey. She had arrived at the airport, only to be told politely that the earliest flight was at five in the afternoon.

She had returned to the house then, and had packed her bags. Then she had done what she had dreaded doing; she had explained the situation to Emily, telling her that the engagement was a sham, trying not to point the finger of blame at Grant, which had been difficult since, as far as she was concerned, he was firmly responsible for the whole mess.

'So he didn't ask you to marry him, then, did he?' Emily had asked, to which she had been forced to reply that he had.

She tried now not to think of that disappointed, accusing little face. She had seen all too clearly what Emily had been thinking. That, all said and done, her father had proposed marriage to Roberta and she had refused. Young minds thought on simple terms. Emily had grasped what she had considered the essentials and had silently left Roberta to finish her packing, her eyes glassy with tears.

She couldn't understand that driving need Roberta had felt to get out. How could she? Roberta had held that information to herself, trying to justify her refusal in terms that Emily would be able to understand, but it had been an impossible task. At the bottom of all those anxious pleas for understanding, Emily had just comprehended the stark denial. She was only fourteen, after all.

How much Roberta had wished that she could explain it all rationally, define the grey in between the black and white, but she couldn't. She was hardly able to come to terms with it herself.

The situation which she had vigorously argued with herself could be controlled had suddenly become overpowering and unmanageable, like some great wild animal that had broken out of its cage and was running amok.

She had seduced Grant and had seen in one dreadful, blinding flash that she could no longer keep up the pretence of imagining that her love for him was something that could be handled with the same aplomb with which she had handled everything else in her life.

Even after her affair with Brian she had quickly picked up the reins of her life, gritted her teeth together, and made a show of carrying on as normal. It had been eating her up inside, but that she had been able to keep to herself.

It frightened her that she was not allowed the luxury of even that with Grant. He had swept into her, minutely burrowing into every pore of her being, until her eyes and actions said what she knew her lips should conceal.

Things, though, always seemed different in the light of day. The frantic nightmares receded, replaced by mundane practicality and logic.

As the taxi fought a losing battle with the traffic, she wondered whether she should have stayed put, grinned and borne it all for a bit longer.

What must the Ishikomos think of her? She didn't like to imagine. She had left a brief note for Grant, telling him that she had left and that she didn't want him to follow her. And he hadn't. No doubt he had provided an adequate explanation to his hosts for her unexpected, rude departure. He was good at lying, wasn't he?

Then she wondered about Grant. How would he have reacted at her disappearance? He wouldn't have gone mad, not as a guest in someone else's house. No doubt he would have viewed it with cold contempt, final proof of her cowardice.

That, more than anything else, hurt. The time had come to put all thoughts of him to the dark recesses of her mind, she knew that, but right now the wound was still too raw, and images of him whirled around in her head until she could have wept with miserable frustration.

She looked around her vacantly. Nothing at all had changed, which seemed odd considering how much she had changed. Life went on, though, didn't it? She would get herself a job; she might even stop doing au pair work altogether and do a course in something useful like computer programming. It might do her good to hold down a normal job, to work normal hours, to have a normal social life.

Her friends, at any rate, would be pleased. She never seemed to see as much of them as she wanted to.

A fortnight later, she was beginning to wonder whether changing jobs had been such a good idea after all. For starters, she had not made much of a hit at the employment agencies with her lack of experience. They had all said the same thing—leave it with us, we'll try our best—but in these days of recession companies were cutting back, they were shedding staff, and the few vacancies going in the areas she had specified were for experienced people.

And Roberta had been in no mood to sell herself to reluctant men and women in starched suits who read her CV with rueful expressions.

The fact was that she had lost interest in everything. She cleaned the house when she could no longer put up with accumulated layers of clothing listlessly dropped on the floor; she snacked on whatever she happened to chance upon whenever she happened to be hungry, and was losing weight, and the friends whom she had promised faithfully to call as soon as she returned to England were still on her list of those things to do which never seemed to get done.

Today, at least, had been better than most. She had been to an interview for a job as a trainee computer operator. The pay was hardly staggering but, in view of her lack of choice, she knew that she would have to accept the post should it be offered to her. The thought depressed her.

She opened her front door, not bothering to switch on the lights, and walked towards the window, pulling shut the curtains, then sank on to the sofa and closed her eyes.

Tomorrow, she thought. I'll definitely ring Amanda. Staying in every night, trying to watch television, was beginning to drive her mad.

She remembered that she had forgotten to buy anything to eat and groaned.

Then he spoke, his voice cutting through the room like a pistol shot, making her sit bolt upright in stunned surprise.

'You hardly seem on top of the world.' The same laconic voice that had been playing mercilessly in her head ever since she had arrived back from Toronto.

Roberta ran to the switch and turned on the lights; then she stared, not believing her eyes.

'I can't be seeing this,' she muttered, blinking, and he drawled drily,

'Depends. Tell me what you think you're seeing and I'll tell you whether you're hallucinating or not.'

But she knew exactly what she was seeing. Grant was just as she had remembered him. He was dressed casually in dark trousers and a dark, thick jumper and he was sitting on the armchair in the corner of the room.

She should have seen him as soon as she had entered the house, but she hadn't even looked in that direction. In fact, she had been so wrapped up in her thoughts that she doubted she had seen anything. Her instinct to draw the curtains together was automatic.

'What are you doing here?' she whispered, walking uncomfortably towards the sofa, over-aware of those unforgettable green eyes on her, and perching uncomfortably on the edge. 'How did you get in?'

'Your neighbour let me in,' Grant said smoothly. There was some underlying hesitation in his manner, which she guessed at rather than saw, as if he was not quite as controlled as he was trying to make her think he was.

He stood up, flexing his arms, and began to prowl around the room, and suddenly Roberta's shock gave way to anger.

Why had he come? Did it matter, anyway? Maybe he was in London on business and he had thought that he would look her up for old times' sake. He had mentioned once that he was quite often in this part of the world.

Whatever the reason, she had not invited him here, and she didn't want him in her house. This was her sanctuary. He would taint it with his presence. She would never be able to look at the ornaments, the bric-à-brac, without her head filling up with images of him inspecting it all.

'She had no right,' Roberta informed him in a high, tight voice. 'She can't just go letting any and everybody into my house. I'll speak to her about that!'

'I explained who I was,' Grant pointed out, inspecting the pictures on the walls, the books on the bookshelf, then moving across to the window against which he proceeded to lounge indolently and resume his inspection of her.

'I don't care! That's not the point!'

'No, it's not, is it?'

There was a thick silence in the room, and Roberta met his stare with a slightly frantic expression. The palms of her hands were damp with perspiration and she wiped them against her skirt.

'Then what is?' Why had she asked? He had been waiting for that question; she could see it in the flicker of his eyes.

'Why did you run out on me?'

She had known that he was going to ask her that, and she had no answer to it, so she stared at him in silence, drinking in the long lines of his body, feeling like someone who had suddenly come upon an oasis after weeks of wandering in a desert.

She didn't want to feel this way, but she couldn't help herself.

'I asked you a question,' he said softly, folding his arms across his chest.

Roberta's fingers twined together on her lap. 'I couldn't put up with...things...any longer.'

At that his face hardened. 'You mean you found me that unbearable to be with? You could bring yourself to make love to me, but you couldn't bear the thought of waking up to me?' She didn't answer and he continued harshly, 'Emily misses you. She hasn't said so, but she's withdrawn into her shell. She hardly speaks to her grandmother and she doesn't speak to me at all.'

'I'm sorry,' Roberta whispered.

He moved towards her swiftly and sat down on the sofa next to her.

'Is that all you can say?' he demanded grimly. 'You're sorry?'

'What else do you want me to say?' She looked away uncomfortably and he dragged her face towards him, forcing her to look at him.

The feel of his fingers on her skin was like little electric currents and she winced.

'Marry me.'

'For Emily's sake?'

He looked away and nodded. 'Something like that,' he muttered roughly.

'I can't.' Her voice was steadier now, even though her heart was still thumping madly in her chest.

'Why not?'

'I can't marry without love,' she said quietly, and before she could finish he interrupted with an angry growl.

'You mean you loved that bastard who fleeced you of your money?'

'No!' Roberta protested.

'But you would have married him?'

'Yes, but——'

'Then how come the sudden onset of principles with me? Does Emily mean that little to you?'

'You know she doesn't!' Roberta flared up angrily. 'You're twisting everything around. I didn't marry Brian... I thought I loved him; I was wrong.'

'You love Emily, don't you?'

She nodded, and immediately felt as though she had stepped into a trap which had been cleverly set to trip her up just when she least expected it.

'Did you come all this way to ask me that?'

'I love my daughter.'

'So much so that you would enter a loveless marriage with me?'

He looked away from her at that, and the discomfort that she had guessed at earlier was more apparent now.

'I find,' he said heavily, still not looking at her, 'I find that I seem to need you as well.'

She looked at him in confusion and astonishment. He needed her. Was that his way of saying that he wanted her? It certainly didn't have anything to do with love.

'But you don't love me,' she muttered dully. 'You'll never love me or anyone else. You gave your wife your love and you'll never have any left over to give anyone else.'

'Does that matter so much to you?' He was staring at her with interest now, and Roberta flushed.

'Emily needs a mother,' she said, lifting her chin mutinously, 'and all right, perhaps you're attracted to me.' She gave a dry, humourless laugh. 'Or perhaps you're just attracted to the ghost of your wife that you see in me.'

'You're talking rubbish!'

'Am I? That night in the cabin, when we made love. Would it have happened if I hadn't been wearing that nightshirt of your wife's? Would it have happened if, for just one minute, I hadn't reminded you of her?' When he didn't answer, she continued relentlessly, 'I'll never be a substitute! I'll never let myself be used by anyone again. Can't you try and understand that?'

'Why do you insist on dragging my wife into all this?'

'Because——'

He held up one hand. 'Let me explain about Vivian,' he said in a low, weary voice. 'Yes, I can't deny that when I first saw you, it was a shock.' She opened her mouth to interrupt and he said harshly, 'Let me finish. You had the same sweet, vulnerable-looking face, those wide grey eyes, that bright hair.' He reached out and gathered her hair in his hand, trailing it through his fingers like water, and it was all she could do not to pull back.

Part of her didn't want to hear this at all, but another part longed to with almost masochistic yearning.

'I fell in love with that same sweet face,' he said heavily. 'We were both very young, and it didn't occur to me to look any further than what I could see. You don't, do you, when you're nothing more than a kid?'

'And?' Roberta prompted when he didn't speak.

He let her hair fall and sat back, staring upwards at the ceiling. 'And I didn't see the obvious. That, sure, she was attracted to me, but she was far more attracted to my money. I was rich then; I had inherited a vast sum on my father's death. My own career was already beginning to take off and I was hungry for success. She recognised the potential for wealth and that was what drew her to me. We got married and almost immediately things began to go downhill. She wanted all the trappings of the high life and she was determined to get them. She threw massive parties. Her sweet vulnerability fell away to reveal the determined, avaricious woman that she was. She had countless affairs and I withdrew from her. But by then we had had Emily, and she threatened to ensure that I would have no visiting rights if I divorced her. I was in a Catch 22 situation.' He sighed. 'I lived with her and I loathed her. I've never said this to another living soul, but it was a relief when she was killed in that road accident. So when I saw you I reacted; well, I over-reacted. But of course you weren't like her at all. Nothing like her. You have no idea how I fought what I felt for you.'

'And what did you feel?' Roberta asked in a small voice.

'I was attracted to you,' he said heavily. 'You know that. You probably knew it from the very start. You're shrewd.'

'That's a dubious compliment.' She gave him a wan smile.

'I told myself that you were probably just like the rest of the female species. Born manipulators. But it didn't help. I was still so damned attracted to you that it was eating me up.'

Roberta's skin was burning, and she had to remind herself that lust and love were poles apart, but when he was so close to her, and after what seemed like such a long time, forever, she could hardly think straight. All she had to do was to stretch out her hand and she would be able to touch him, to feel that hard, bronzed body that had driven her mad in Toronto, and had finally driven her out.

He reached out his hand and stroked the side of her face, and her breath caught in her throat.

'Attraction's not enough,' she said, drawing away, but he caught her and pulled her towards him, his lips touching her face with tiny, hungry kisses that made her whimper.

She put her hands flat against his chest to push him away, but she never got that far because the gentle insistence of his lips on her face became a fierce, demanding kiss on her mouth, an onslaught that left her breathless.

She moved her hands behind his head, pulling him hungrily towards her, feeling the pressure of his body on hers as they both tumbled into a lying position on the sofa. He was too long for it, though, and in a quick movement he lifted her off and carried her towards her bedroom, knowing where it was almost by instinct, kicking shut the door.

'I want you to marry me, Roberta,' he said huskily, his hand moving to free her from her clothes, expertly unbuttoning her blouse and tossing it on to the floor. 'You're beautiful. You've been in my head since I set eyes on you, do you know that?' His voice was unsteady.

He unclasped her lacy bra and her breasts spilled out, rising and falling quickly as her breathing became erratic.

He cupped one breast in his hand and said unevenly, 'I discover that I seem to be in love with you.'

Roberta held her breath. 'Could you repeat that?'

'I wasn't looking for love,' he said accusingly, and her pink mouth curved into a slight smile. 'After Vivian, I had made up my mind that love was something I could well do without. I told myself over and over that you were a challenge, that I just wanted to get behind that prim English façade of yours, that it was nothing more than that. Whenever I thought of you I had that gut-wrenching excitement that adolescents get when they think they're in love. I never felt that way even with Vivian. I reasoned that it was because you were so different from the women I had gone out with before. You had a way of looking, almost as if you were laughing at me, and it made me furious and excited at the same time.' He smoothed his hand along her stomach and bent to kiss the warmth between her breasts. 'Please marry me,' he whispered. 'I don't think I could live my life without you.'

'How could I refuse your proposal when you put it like that?' Roberta teased, her eyes serious. 'I longed for you to tell me that what you felt was more than just a passing attraction.'

'Do you know,' Grant murmured sheepishly, 'that at one point I thought that you were still in love with that bastard, even though you denied it?'

'Brian?' She laughed ruefully. 'I was never in love with him. I knew that for sure the minute you arrived on the scene. It made what I felt for Brian seem like a passing crush. But he was like your wife, in a way. He ruined the male sex for me. When I came to Toronto it was to get away, and I was absolutely determined not to get involved with another man again.'

'But you couldn't resist me.' Grant gave her a wicked, crooked smile. 'I seem to have that effect on the opposite sex.'

Roberta laughed at that, then she said soberly, 'If I marry you, I don't want you to even glance in the direction of another woman.'

'I'll make sure that I keep my eyes averted even when I'm talking to my mother. Who, incidentally, already likes you. She was beginning to get a little tired of my lack of serious involvement.'

'She told you that?'

'Not in so many words. But I was subjected to her pet lectures on men who go through life unmarried and end up as fussy, cranky old bores with eccentric habits.'

'I'll make sure you don't go that way,' Roberta assured him, thinking that that was one thing he could never become, even if he spent the rest of his days locked in a room, as a confirmed bachelor.

He gave a low laugh, hardly hearing her as his mouth found her breasts and roused one nipple into aching hardness. Then he guided her hand to his arousal, his breathing thick as she stroked him. He kissed her on her neck, massaging the fullness of her breasts with his hands while his thumbs continued their erotic teasing of her nipples. Then he trailed a path along her stomach with his finger, pausing to circle her navel.

Roberta arched back, parting her legs to his exploring fingers, wriggling against him as he caressed her intimately, keeping his hand there when he would have removed it to linger on the silken smoothness of her thighs.

She heard him groan against her neck, and when he raised his dark head to look at her passionately she knew exactly what he was thinking.

It had been weeks since they had last made love. He was as desperate for her as she was for him.

He moved into her and she shuddered convulsively, wrapping her legs around his thighs, her body responding to his with instinctive rhythm. There was something savage and hungry in the way he brought her to the shuddering peak of her arousal.

And now there was an element to their lovemaking that had not hitherto been present. This time she was not clutching to herself the awful suspicion that he wanted her body for all the wrong reasons.

Later, when they were lying in each other's arms, she said softly, 'Did you think that I would agree to marry you when you showed up here? It took an awful lot of courage.'

He looked at her through drowsy green eyes. 'I would have forced you,' he said calmly.

'You would have forced me?'

'Dragged you kicking and screaming to the nearest Register Office.'

'Register Office? Not on your life! At least, not without your darling daughter there. I don't think she would ever forgive me. And, anyway, I can't believe that you would have done that,' she teased. 'Would you really?' She gave a throaty chuckle. 'I had no idea you were into the caveman approach.'

'I wasn't. Not until I met you. I blame you entirely.' He grinned. 'I was absolutely determined to have you. Do you know,' he confessed, 'that when I was with the Ishikomos I deliberately trapped you into that situation?'

'You didn't!' She looked at him in surprise. 'I thought it was a convenient excuse.'

'Well, a man has got some pride,' he said huskily. 'I wasn't sure how you felt about me. I knew that you were attracted to me——'

'Like the rest of the female species, geriatrics included,' she said, raising one eyebrow.

'So you admit my universal sex appeal.' He threw her a teasing smile. 'Anyway, I knew that you wanted me, but you were so adamant about not getting involved that I figured that if I coerced you by hook or by crook into marrying me, I could work on you. I was determined to use every ploy in the book to get you to go through with it. I might have guessed that you wouldn't let yourself get railroaded into my plans, though.'

'Devious swine,' Roberta said contentedly. 'And if I had known the reasons behind your offer, your business arrangement, I might well have let myself get railroaded into it. It never even crossed my mind that you would do anything like that for me, or anyone else for that matter.'

'When it comes to you, I'll do anything. Don't you think that sounds pathetic?'

'I think it sounds promising.' She stroked him, feeling him stir against her hand, and closed her eyes.

Yesterday seemed like a decade ago, and tomorrow was opening up for them like a rosebud unfurling its petals under the first rays of sun.

Now, she thought, she would never have to run again.

4 FREE

Romances
and 2 FREE gifts
just for you!

*You can enjoy all the
heartwarming emotion of true love for FREE!
Discover the heartbreak and the happiness, the emotion and
the tenderness of the modern relationships in
Mills & Boon Romances.*

*We'll send you 4 captivating Romances as a special offer from
Mills & Boon Reader Service, along with the chance to have
6 Romances delivered to your door each month.*

Claim your FREE books and gifts ~~ov~~

An irresistible offer from Mills & Boon

Here's a personal invitation from Mills & Boon Reader Service, to become a regular reader of Romances. To welcome you, we'd like you to have 4 books, a CUDDLY TEDDY and a special MYSTERY GIFT absolutely FREE.

Then you could look forward each month to receiving 6 brand new Romances, delivered to your door, postage and packing free! Plus our free Newsletter featuring author news, competitions, special offers and much more.

This invitation comes with no strings attached. You may cancel or suspend your subscription at any time, and still keep your free books and gifts.

It's so easy. Send no money now. Simply fill in the coupon below and post it to -
Reader Service, FREEPOST,
PO Box 236, Croydon, Surrey CR9 9EL.

NO STAMP REQUIRED

Free Books Coupon

Yes! Please rush me 4 free Romances and 2 free gifts! Please also reserve me a Reader Service subscription. If I decide to subscribe I can look forward to receiving 6 brand new Romances each month for just £10.20, postage and packing free. If I choose not to subscribe I shall write to you within 10 days - I can keep the books and gifts whatever I decide. I may cancel or suspend my subscription at any time. I am over 18 years of age.

Ms/Mrs/Miss/Mr_____ EP31R

Address_____

_____

Postcode_____Signature _____

Offer expires 31st May 1993. The right is reserved to refuse an application and change the terms of this offer. Readers overseas and ~~ire~~ please send for details. Southern Africa write to Book ~~International Ltd, P.O. Box 42654, Craighall, Transvaal 2024.~~ ~~...led~~ with offers from other reputable companies as a

...re in this opportunity, please tick box ☐

...erleaf...

Forthcoming Titles

DUET
Available in April

The Penny Jordan Duet　　**LOVING**
　　　　　　　　　　　　　　TOO SHORT A BLESSING

The Roberta Leigh Duet　　**NO MAN'S MISTRESS**
　　　　　　　　　　　　　　AN IMPOSSIBLE MAN TO LOVE

BEST SELLER ROMANCE
Available in May

THE SWEETEST TRAP Robyn Donald
NO LONGER A DREAM Carole Mortimer

MEDICAL ROMANCE
Available in May

THE CONSTANT HEART Judith Ansell
JOEL'S WAY Abigail Gordon
PRIDE'S FALL Flora Sinclair
ONLY THE LONELY Judith Worthy

Next Month's Romances

Each month you can choose from a wide variety of romance with Mills & Boon. Below are the new titles to look out for next month, why not ask either Mills & Boon Reader Service or your Newsagent to reserve you a copy of the titles you want to buy — just tick the titles you would like and either post to Reader Service or take it to any Newsagent and ask them to order your books.

Please save me the following titles:		Please tick	√
HIGH RISK	Emma Darcy		
PAGAN SURRENDER	Robyn Donald		
YESTERDAY'S ECHOES	Penny Jordan		
PASSIONATE CAPTIVITY	Patricia Wilson		
LOVE OF MY HEART	Emma Richmond		
RELATIVE VALUES	Jessica Steele		
TRAIL OF LOVE	Amanda Browning		
THE SPANISH CONNECTION	Kay Thorpe		
SOMETHING MISSING	Kate Walker		
SOUTHERN PASSIONS	Sara Wood		
FORGIVE AND FORGET	Elizabeth Barnes		
YESTERDAY'S DREAMS	Margaret Mayo		
STORM OF PASSION	Jenny Cartwright		
MIDNIGHT STRANGER	Jessica Marchant		
WILDER'S WILDERNESS	Miriam Macgregor		
ONLY TWO CAN SHARE	Annabel Murray		

If you would like to order these books in addition to your regular subscription from Mills & Boon Reader Service please send £1.80 per title to: Mills & Boon Reader Service, Freepost, P.O. Box 236, Croydon, Surrey, CR9 9EL, quote your Subscriber No:.................................... (If applicable) and complete the name and address details below. Alternatively, these books are available from many local Newsagents including W.H.Smith, J.Menzies, Martins and other paperback stockists from 14th May 1993.

Name:...

Address:...

....Post Code:...........................

Retailer: If you would like to stock M&B books please .... your regular book/magazine wholesaler for details.

.... with offers from other reputable companies as a result of this application. .... advantage of these opportunities please tick box ☐